Lake Like a Mirror

Lake Like a Mirror

Ho Sok Fong

Translated from Chinese by Natascha Bruce

TWO LINES
PRESS

Two Lines Press
582 Market Street, Suite 700, San Francisco, CA 94104
www.twolinespress.com

ISBN 978-1-931883-98-6

Library of Congress Cataloging-in-Publication Data
Names: Ho Sok Fong, author. | Bruce, Natascha, translator.
Title: Lake Like a Mirror / Ho Sok Fong; translated from the Chinese by
Natascha Bruce.
Description: San Francisco: Two Lines Press, 2020.
Identifiers: LCCN 2019034371 (print) | LCCN 2019034372 (ebook) | ISBN
9781931883986 (paperback) | ISBN 9781931883993 (ebook)
Subjects: LCSH: Ho Sok Fong--Translations into English.
Classification: LCC PL2937.5.O64 A2 2020 (print) | LCC PL2937.5.O64
(ebook) | DDC 895.13/6--dc23
LC record available at https://lccn.loc.gov/2019034371
LC ebook record available at https://lccn.loc.gov/2019034372

Cover design by Gabriele Wilson
Cover photo © Cig Harvey
Design by Sloane | Samuel

Printed in the United States of America

1 3 5 7 9 10 8 6 4 2

This book is supported in part by an award from the National
Endowment for the Arts.

Contents

The Wall

WHEN THE DEVELOPERS said they were building a wall to keep out the sound, everybody thought it was a good idea. For the past few years, the expressway had been expanding, coming closer and closer to our houses. It used to be a full sixty meters away, but now had come so close we were practically run over every time we opened our back doors.

One morning, a seven-year-old girl really was run over outside her back door. Late that night, the developers started building a wall along the side of the road.

"They're laying bricks straight onto the ground," said the aunty next door. From her upstairs window, she watched the workmen spread a layer of cement, then position a line of bricks, then smear on more cement.

"It's got no foundations," she said to her husband, when she came back downstairs. He was watching a football game on television, and when they scored he clapped and cheered with the South American sportscaster, so didn't hear her.

His wife wasn't surprised. She went back to watching

the workmen build the wall. She thought they looked thin, as though they were too feeble for a job like that. But their wall looked very thick, thick enough to hide one of them in it. It grew higher and higher, until it blocked her view. When it was over one story high, she went to bed.

The next morning, all the tenants in our row woke to find the wall was finished. It cut off the sunlight, making our back gardens and kitchens dark. But everybody agreed that sunlight wasn't much of a price to pay, considering the seven-year-old girl who'd been killed by a car. The only thing was, the wall blocked our back doors too, and now they opened only a little wider than the width of a foot. Wide enough for a cat, or a small dog, but too much of a squeeze for a human.

The next-door aunty wasn't happy. Wasn't this the same as having no back door at all? No back door meant no way out. Her husband agreed. "It's like having a mouth but no asshole," is what he said.

But, gradually, they got used to it. There's nothing a person can't get used to. It wasn't too much of a hardship, anyway, not compared to what that girl's mother was going through. Two days after the incident, the aunty and her husband saw a tiny coffin being carried out through the other family's gate. A few days later, the mother lit a fire in a big metal trashcan by her front door and burned her daughter's clothes and schoolbag. The thick white smoke reeked of melting plastic and choked up the whole street.

The aunty couldn't remember if her husband had ever left the house. He sat glued to the football on the television. The light was gone from their windows, but they carried on as best they could.

The aunty had no kids to take care of and spent most of her time in the kitchen. If she closed the kitchen door, she couldn't even hear the television. Before the wall, the kitchen had been filled with the roar of cars hurtling along the expressway. After the wall, the noise was muffled, like a person humming deep within their chest. After a few days, she was used to it, and didn't mind much one way or the other.

She did do things a little differently after the wall. It blocked the sunlight, making her eyes too tired to read the newspaper. Instead, she turned her attention to her tiny garden, about the size of a toilet stall, just next to the kitchen. In the first week she planted cacti, and later added dumb canes, bush lilies, hydrangeas, and gerbera daisies, filling the little space to bursting. You'd have been impressed, if you'd seen it—big fat leaves springing from such a tiny patch of soil, spreading out so that there was almost nowhere left to stand. And it seemed to be because of the wall: the gloom meant the soil stayed moist and the plants flourished. In addition to the plants in her garden, the aunty kept a bowl of goldfish in the kitchen.

Her husband hardly ever came into the kitchen, so he didn't know she also kept a fluffy tabby cat. He'd had a lung infection a while before, and had been wary of dog and cat hair ever since. The cat had sneaked in the day after the wall went up. The aunty had been trying to push open the back door, and it had squeezed through that sliver of a gap. She guessed the cat belonged to one of the houses farther down the row, and that, because her slightly opened door had barred its way, it had decided that it might as well come in. It leaped boldly onto a chair, then strolled right into her little garden, where it relieved itself. After that, she couldn't bring herself to put it back outside again. She hugged it close, feeling its weight against her, like the weight of the loneliness in the pit of her stomach.

Because of the goldfish, she had to keep the cat shut away in the garden. She couldn't let it inside, but neither could she let it leave. It often fell asleep out there. When it woke up it would prowl around in circles, and when it was hungry it would rub against the door, meowing. She was careful never to feed it too much: if it was hungry, it needed her. She felt there was an invisible rope between them, and when the cat was hungry, the rope pulled taut. At first, she'd thought about finding a real rope to tie the cat up with, but then she'd decided that as long as she shut the door tightly things would be fine as they were.

One morning, while she was out shopping, her husband went into the kitchen. He opened all three doors—to the back alley, to the little garden, and to the rest of the house—and then went back to the living room, where he sat contentedly reading the paper. When his wife came home, she found the goldfish bowl smashed to pieces and water all over the floor. Her husband was just sitting there, without a care in the world.

"What happened to the fishbowl?"

Her husband glanced up, but said nothing.

"And the cat?"

He shrugged. She glared at his expression, hating the

way he acted as though this had nothing to do with him. A chill swept through her chest; bit by bit, she felt her heart turn to ice. And so, when she spoke again, she was even frostier than him: "Cat got your tongue?"

"What are you talking about? Have a cat if you like! Don't ask me!"

He went back to reading his paper, flicking from international news to the sports pages.

"Brazil won!" he exclaimed, delighted. But his cheery tones weren't for his wife's benefit. It was as if there were a crowd in front of him, eagerly awaiting his reaction.

She went back into the kitchen, where she slowly washed radishes and chopped greens. Methodically, she threw pork bones and medicinal herbs into a pot, to brew into a soup. Once she'd finished, she sat down at the table. It didn't feel necessary to do anything else but think. In the afternoon, she put a saucer of fish and rice in the back alley and left the door open. She waited for a whole day, but the cat did not come back. She strained her ears, but couldn't hear even the faintest meow.

A few days later, she thought she heard the cat crying, the way it did when it hadn't had enough to eat. She sat in the kitchen but couldn't figure out where the sound was coming from. For a while, she suspected it might be right there in the little garden, because the cries seemed to be coming from the cluster of dumb canes and bush lilies. She stayed in the kitchen for a long time, with the doors and the back window open, but saw no sign of the cat.

She closed the doors.

After a while, her husband came into the kitchen. He

had the feeling it'd been quite some time since he'd seen her. He stared at her blankly and, after a long pause, said, "You got thin."

She didn't react. He walked over to the back door. He'd been planning on opening the door to let the breeze in, but the moment he tried his face puckered in disgust. "It stinks! What is it, a dead rat?"

He slammed the door shut.

After her husband left, she studied herself carefully and discovered it was true: she was thin. She walked to the back door and found she was almost thin enough to squeeze through the gap. This was not bad at all, she thought—a few more days and she'd be able to fit right through.

And a few days later, that's exactly what she did. She walked along the back alley, which was not much wider than the gap in the door, and felt happy and carefree. She pressed an ear to the wall, and could feel it shake as endless numbers of cars rushed past, rumbling like waves against a shore. She could hear their engines, their wheels grinding against the pavement; they seemed to thrum within the wall itself like the surge of blood inside a body. She pressed her emaciated palm against the wall and felt the vibrations coming through, beating against the veins on the back of her hand. She pressed her other palm to the wall and felt the fingers of both hands trembling like withered dumb cane leaves. She inched her whole body up to the wall, pressing her bony legs against it, and shook like a feathery bamboo.

She continued her walk. The sky above her was a murky gray and the alley was a hideous mess. She hadn't expected that it would accumulate so much litter in so little time. She saw styrofoam takeout boxes, chicken bones, fish bones, eggshells, cooked rice, bread, sticky clumps of discarded meals, nails, clothes, school bags, pencil cases, leather handbags, bricks, shovels, cassette tapes, CDs, soup spoons, flowerpots, glass bottles, pillows, shoes, tires, magazines, newspapers, flies. She couldn't bear the thought of the cat picking through all this trash. She began to feel like she was in a graveyard with no one in charge and rotting corpses strewn all over the place, and realized that this must be the source of that stink her husband had complained about.

As she stepped over the pieces of litter, she noticed the lightness of her body; not even the styrofoam boxes were crushed beneath her feet. She stooped to peer inside the tires, thinking they'd be a likely place for a cat to hide. Feeling frail, she moved very slowly, worried her bones had become too fragile and might snap. Those bones still needed to hold her up. Her whole frame felt on the verge of collapse.

She stopped sharing a bedroom with her husband and put a thin mattress on the kitchen floor. A thin bed for a thin person. Too thick and soft a mattress would have made it hard for her to sit up. But because she was so thin, she was more aware than ever of the feeling in each part of her body. A sensation of hot or cold in her chest spread rapidly to her back, then swiftly through her limbs to her fingers and toes. Nothing stayed in one place. She felt everything more thoroughly and intensely than before. She quite liked it.

The aunty kept looking for the cat, but found her memories evaporating, becoming increasingly less defined. Did the cat have three patches on its forehead, or four? Was the tip of its tail black, or brown? Sometimes she even wondered whether she'd really been out of the house the morning the cat went missing. And which had come first, the cat or the goldfish? The cat or the wall? Did the goldfish bowl have goldfish in it? How many? She couldn't remember the details. But as the memories grew hazier, she found herself less and less sad—quite relaxed, to tell the truth. It felt nice.

One day, the aunty sneaked into our house like a cat. My mom had opened our back door. She was holding a bag of trash, ready to chuck it into the alley, as the aunty walked by. The door blocked her way, so she stepped inside. My little brother and I watched, wide-eyed, as she strolled casually into our kitchen. She was the thinnest person we'd ever seen, like one of the paper figures we used to shut inside our books and hide in our desk drawers at school, except she was as tall as we were, and she wasn't pretty. The paper dolls were all little girls with blue eyes and blonde hair, but she was old and ugly, with a face full of wrinkles.

"Such sweet children, how nice!" she said to our mom, her eyes sliding over me and my brother. We were playing with our toy trains.

She said this, but she stood back from us and didn't come closer, as though afraid we'd snap her in two. When she spoke, we could see the air passing magically over her throat, making her vocal chords quiver like violin strings. Concerned, our mom asked how she'd gotten so thin, and the aunty answered that she wasn't sure herself. Maybe because she'd been chasing after a cat, she said. She remembered loving the cat, but sadly not what color it was.

They were still talking when our dad came home from working at the hospital. When he saw the state the aunty was in, his jaw dropped so far that it seemed he'd barely be able to close it again. He led her into his office, where he took her blood pressure and listened to her heartbeat. He said you could hear her heart just as clearly through her back as through her chest, and you could almost see it beating, even through her clothes. It was inconceivable. "The Creator works in mysterious ways," he said.

The aunty came to our house a few more times after that, and told us something different each time. She said she'd been planting things. She talked about how enormous spiders lurked in their cobwebs between the plants. She said she'd just planted a carnivorous pitcher plant, and the soil back there was so moist that the plant had sprouted pitchers big enough to swallow a person.

When she came over, my brother and I held our noses because she stank like a dead rat. Our mom and dad put up with it, but after she left they always said they felt sick. Dad tried hard to convince her to come to the hospital for a check-up, but she claimed she couldn't be bothered. "I'm OK," she said. "I've lived enough."

Dad frowned. Once, I heard him grumbling to our mom, saying that they'd have to set up a video camera in the aunty's house because it was truly a mystery how she stayed alive at all.

We don't know whether he followed through with this plan, because of what happened next. One evening, a truck smashed into the wall, sending it crashing down. We'd been asleep upstairs and felt our beds and the whole house shake.

Our garden was buried under little mountains of bricks, and half the kitchen was gone. Dad was afraid the rest of the house would collapse too, and sent us to spend the night with our grandma. As we were leaving, we saw workmen arriving, dispatched by the developers.

We only stayed with our grandma for one night. When we came back the next afternoon, there was no sign of the wall, not even a fragment of brick. They'd cleared it all away overnight. Once again, we had an unobstructed view of the traffic racing down the expressway. A stray dog came running down what used to be the narrow alley alongside the wall. It was hard to imagine this empty space as the filthy alley the aunty was always talking about. We couldn't see her pitcher plant. The aunty herself had disappeared.

When the aunty had been gone for several months, an old stray dog raked the soil with its front paws, howling in excitement, and pulled out a ball of fluff, crawling with maggots. At first, we couldn't figure out what it was. Then we saw the brown-and-black striped fur, and we shouted in alarm: "Cat! Aunty's dead cat!"

An old man poked his head out of an upstairs window. He hurried down, exclaimed in surprise, and said, as if it had just occurred to him: "So that's it! That's where she had the pitcher plant."

He bent over, leaning close to us with his liver-spotted face. There were cobwebs stuck to his collar. He said, "A pitcher plant can eat a person! It ate Aunty. You scared?"

We slipped back into the house. The aunty had been eaten by her own pitcher plant. We couldn't form the words to tell anyone.

When she appeared in our dreams, she was as thin as a moth's wing. She insisted that she wasn't dead.

"Your husband says you are!" we said, and she snorted in contempt.

Her complexion merged slowly into the gray of the wall and it seemed that the gloom all around us was her camouflage.

Later, we dreamed about her being devoured by her pitcher plant.

After that, we never dreamed of her again.

Radio Drama

"They then call to each other like people lost in a wood."
— Nietzsche, *Human, All Too Human*

"THE POLICE ARE OUTSIDE."

"In blue uniforms?"

"No, white ones."

"What are they doing?"

"Directing traffic. Someone died and the funeral's about to start. Cars are parked everywhere."

"We had to drive around for ages before we found a spot."

A pause.

"Are the police here a lot?"

"I'd say so. Always driving in, strolling around, poking about. Who knows what they're looking for."

"Have they ever questioned you?"

"No, no, absolutely not."

My mother stood staring out of the window. Eventually, she came back over and sat down. There was only one hairdresser in the salon and so everyone had to wait their turn. The room reeked of hair gel. A thick bank of hair clippings lay across the floor like a glossy black pelt.

The hairdresser combed out a handful of a girl's hair, then snipped it off.

"Such gorgeous hair," she cooed.

The flattery had no effect on the girl, who was completely wooden, sitting as though tied up with an invisible rope. Her mother sat behind her, chatting about school, about how the holidays were almost over, and the various new rules and regulations. There were prescribed lengths for fingernails, hair, skirts. Skirts had to be below the knee, she said. Then she moved on to punishments: first a verbal warning, then demerits. It was all very strict. And these things cost time, as well as academic points. The girl was very still beneath the voluminous salon gown, like a tent pegged to the seat, and her hair slid down the tent's canvas like fallen leaves, landing at her feet. She let it fall, acting as if the conversation had nothing to do with her.

"It'll grow back," said the hairdresser. "When it does, you come and see me."

"The school might loosen up," said another woman. "Sometimes they're strict to start with, then they relax."

"Then you can leave it long and style it however you want."

The hairdresser was dressed entirely in bright red, giving her a striking resemblance to Little Red Riding Hood. Her face was very white against her lacy, petal-shaped collar. She trampled back and forth across the pile of black hair, concentrating on the haircut.

She seemed about thirty. Quite pretty, if a little tired-looking. Every so often, she chimed in with the conversation.

From her well-timed gasps and witty retorts, it was clear that she understood everyone's Hokkien, although she replied in an Indonesian-accented Malay. Her Malay was fluent and easy to understand, suggesting that she'd lived here a long time.

The other ladies admired her outfit and she chuckled good-naturedly, crinkling her eyes.

"You haven't been back long. Are you planning to go away again?" she asked me, out of the blue.

I started, unnerved that she knew anything about me.

"We'll see. Depends what comes up," I said, vaguely. I didn't have a definite answer.

A little later, I finally remembered where I knew her from. About four years earlier, I'd been home for the university holidays and she had come around to call on my younger sister. Her accent was stronger then.

"She's not here," I'd said, in Malay. Then I'd gone back to my books.

Aside from that fleeting encounter, I drew a blank. Why was she in this salon, ushering in customers and showing them to their seats? Was she an overseas worker? No, she couldn't be, because I'd heard her discussing the salon with the women earlier.

The women had asked what it cost for a place like this and an old woman sitting off to one side answered, "Over a hundred thousand."

The women gasped. "That much! Does she own it? What's the interest on the mortgage?"

The hairdresser cut in. "No interest, it was paid for in cash."

"And how much to fix it up?"

"Around forty thousand," said the hairdresser. "It was just a room. There was a wall here and I knocked it down to open up the space."

So it was hers. A clean, new, spacious, snow-white salon with its own garden. And because she had this house, this home of her own, she wasn't someone's maid, or a helper in a restaurant or a hawker stand. She wasn't beholden to anyone. Which would mean she was the boss. Yes, she was definitely the boss—how could she be anything else, if she was making a living out of a place that belonged to her? I wasn't sure of the relationship between her and the old woman. And I didn't understand how she could have afforded all this. The house, the big shiny mirror, the row of wheelie chairs and hood dryers, the renovations. I couldn't even afford an apartment.

The hairdresser laughed at the other women's jokes. She made her own easy additions to news of goings-on in Lemon River Town, in a way that made her seem more a part of the place than I was. I felt like an eavesdropping outsider. She seemed to be just like them, with their children, mothers-in-law, and husbands, all belonging to the same small town. I'd been away too long and now there were Lemon River folk I didn't recognize, and names I'd never heard before. I had no idea how things worked anymore.

In a corner of the room, there was a table plastered with banknotes, and on the table was a radio, hardly bigger than my palm. I started fiddling with the dial, trying to change the channel. The speaker was like a deformed mouth, crystal-clear one moment, fuzzy and crackling the next.

The women's chatter bored me. Whose kid was earning big money, who'd been swindled, who was in the hospital, who'd been robbed, who had loaned money, who had debts, who'd helped pay whose debts off. Disjointed words and phrases burrowed into my ears, then dripped out in time with the ticking of the clock. The women talked into the mirror, entirely at ease, gossiping, haranguing, pausing every so often to fluff their hair. It made me feel awkward, which was why I had retreated to the corner, where I could no longer see my own reflection.

To amuse myself, I started to fantasize that they were all nursing deep, dark secrets that, sooner or later, would have to come to light. I listened to scrambled fragments of the afternoon news and pop songs, with one ear still tuned to the women. Their voices masked the crackle of the radio as it searched for a wavelength. At some point, I gave up adjusting the dial.

The radio broadcast a short news bulletin about a missing person. A few years back, a man had gone missing in Lemon River.

The hairdresser spread a large white towel over my mother's shoulders and assessed her hair in the mirror.

"He was such a big man," said my mother. "It's strange they never found him."

"I know, very strange! All this time, and still no sign."

The hairdresser ran her hands through my mother's hair as she spoke.

"What are we doing with it? You want the bangs permed as well?"

"Up to you, just make me look pretty," joked my mother. She looked squarely at her reflection in the mirror, focusing so hard that she seemed to sink inside it, leaving her body behind as a doppelgänger, there to assume the trials of life on her behalf.

"If he got drunk and fell into the river, a body would have floated up. And if he's buried somewhere, they'll dig him up eventually. But if he's alive and in hiding, no chance," said one of the women.

"I heard he's hiding abroad."

"No, that's Ah Tuo."

"Ah Tuo went to Thailand to get away from a creditor."

"How long before the police stop looking?"

"Who knows with them. You want them to look and they won't. You'd rather they didn't, and there they are, making trouble."

The hairdresser said my mother's hair was too brittle for an electric perm but they could try out a new serum, which would curl it without doing any further damage.

"Is that OK?" she asked. "It's only twenty ringgit extra, but it'll take a bit longer."

Her eyes automatically went to me, the grown-up daughter. I nodded, smiling, said, "Sure, no problem."

She beamed.

"We're not in any hurry," I added.

It was true. Neither of us had much going on. My mother no longer had to rush around making lunch for a whole family. I'd been back home, unemployed, for more than six months. The people who used to keep my mother so busy had moved out of her life; even I only flashed in every so often. Why not stay in the salon, looking at ourselves in the mirror and chatting to the other reflections? It was like a scene from one of the soap operas I used to watch as a child on the state television channel. The actors spoke their lines in different languages but seemed to be talking about the same thing—I say "seemed," because I couldn't understand everything, so can't be sure. At the time, I didn't understand why they had to do that. But now, in the salon, I was discovering that people really did talk one language and listen to another. Except, of course, they weren't speaking Malay and Hokkien in the same melodramatic wails as the soap actors. Maybe people only speak like that when they argue.

There was a funeral procession on the next street over. A woman had just left it and come into the salon, and she told us it was for a youngest daughter who had killed herself. Heartbreaking, she said. A year before they had all been at her wedding.

"I heard she had depression."

"What about her husband? Is he there?"

No, he hadn't come. That was strange.

The women made guesses about why that might be. It most likely had to do with a mistress, according to them. But a mistress was only natural, once a man made a bit of money! Nothing strange about that. Most men never had any intention of divorcing their wives; they wouldn't be so stupid. For a wife to kill herself over it, well, that was just silly.

"Life's worth more than that," they pronounced, then

sighed in unison. The thought of such misfortune made them shiver. Adversity: always so much more thrilling than happiness.

In the mirror, I could see that the salon door and windows were tightly closed. The tinted window glass filtered the sun, keeping the room gently shaded. The walls were a spotless white and the floor was covered with pretty blue and white ceramic tiles. Somehow, the whole place felt too new, too airy, too big. There wasn't a single mark on the cream sofa. Outside, there was no shop sign marking the salon. The hairdresser was running the business out of a private home without a license. Some of the women were exclaiming about it: "Really? No license, but you open anyway?"

For the first time, I noticed the bunches of flowers lying in the street outside.

"Can't I invite a few guests over to my own house if I feel like it?" asked the hairdresser.

As far as I could see, the salon was fully equipped. There was a three-tier cart with a little toolbox on top containing razors, combs, and clips in an assortment of sizes. In one corner of the room, there was a hair-washing station, with a reclining chair connected to a white porcelain sink. The usual hairstyle posters were stuck all over the walls. In short, there was every hairdressing item you could think of, in full view. It struck me as odd. If a policeman came knocking at the door, there would be no hiding what was going on.

Time slipped through hair and washed away down the sink.

I looked at the women's reflections. They were spread

along the folding chairs and sofa pressed against the back wall. None seemed willing to come forward and sit in front of the mirror, as if afraid the new wheelie chairs would collapse the moment they sat down. The chairs on either side of my mother were empty, giving the impression that she'd been wheeled on stage for a one-woman performance.

"How long since your husband died?" the old woman asked her.

"Ten years now."

"Well, aren't you something. It's not easy, raising children by yourself."

My mother barely glanced at the other women, keeping her gaze focused on her own face instead. I wondered whether she was seeing something different than what I usually saw; some kind of beauty that she was hoping other people would notice.

"People always say that," she replied. "But I thank my lucky stars I never remarried. I couldn't have faced my kids."

The hairdresser did not join in. She kept her head down, eyes on my mother's hair. She rarely looked in the mirror. It didn't seem to interest her at all. Of course, her job meant that she couldn't avoid it completely, but the few times she did look up, she looked at her clients, never herself. The light cast long shadows beneath her eyes, streaking her cheeks. She twirled locks of hair around her fingers, then twisted them around small rubber curlers. Her fingers were slick with hair lotion, running through my mother's faded, dry hair. Her fingernails seemed to grow longer with every twist. So did the hair.

My mother continued to stare into the mirror, but maybe she wasn't really looking. Maybe she was listening to the drama that had started on the radio, although those kinds of far-off stories are never as gripping as the ones right under your nose. The most interesting secrets are always about people you know.

The old woman disappeared into the kitchen and emerged with a tray of milk jellies, which she began busily handing out to the women. I turned her down, because I find cold foods hard to swallow. The others tucked in.

"You should go out and enjoy yourself," the hairdresser said to my mother.

"Going out costs money," said one woman.

"Get Ah He's god-ma to take you," said another. They all burst out laughing.

"I heard she hits a nightclub every couple of weeks," said yet another. Then she turned to tell me that the milk jelly was delicious and I should try it; the sweet vinegar sprinkled on top made it sweet and sour at the same time.

"It's shocking. Fifty years old if she's a day, still going around in denim miniskirts, dancing a-go-go like a girl half her age."

"Good for her," said the hairdresser.

"Carrying on with all those men, not a thought for what her kids might think."

"We're all different," said my mother. "No harm in having fun, just don't get too carried away. That's when you end up getting cheated."

"Like this friend of my brother-in-law's, she was cheated out of hundreds of thousands of ringgit!"

"Men get carried away too."

"And they get what's coming to them! Broken homes, death, divorce, children all over the place, debts, bankruptcy. Reputations down the drain."

"Like Old Teik's son."

"He's a bad seed all right. Cleaned that family right out, now his poor old dad has to live in a pigeon loft."

"It aged Old Teik to no end. He gave that boy everything."

"And then the boy runs off to England, where apparently he's washing dishes."

"They should pretend he went missing."

"You know that's not how it works. He's rotten, but he's still their son."

The hairdresser wrapped a white towel around my mother's head. Her hands were shaky, and she had to try a few times before she could get it to stay. It was probably the air conditioning. I was cold too, and starting to get hungry.

The conversation wound back to the dead girl with the funeral on the next street over. Such a pity, declared the women.

"After all, it's only natural. What cat doesn't chase mice?"

"So long as he keeps bringing home money, that's the main thing."

"Don't kick up a fuss."

"These things are infatuations, they never last long."

It was as if there were ghosts whispering in the walls.

"You can't take them too seriously."

"No point trying to fix what you can't change."

"Keep it to yourself. If he says nothing, pretend you know nothing."

"You have to learn to turn a blind eye."

"They always come back in the end."

"Do I have to wait much longer?" asked my mother.

The hairdresser nodded. "About half an hour."

She left the room and returned with a broom. She swept the hair trimmings as though reeling in a net, leaving behind an expanse of bright white floor glaring up at us.

"Aren't any of you getting haircuts?" asked my mother.

The women shook their heads.

"Every so often these things drag on. Some men end up bringing their mistresses home with them. And then how is someone supposed to pretend they don't know?" one of them asked.

"I've still got jellies in the fridge, let me get them." The old woman stood up and walked unsteadily to the kitchen.

One of the women inspected her feet. "Look at them," she said. "I don't know what's going on, they get so swollen."

"If you press on them, do your fingers leave marks?" asked another. "If they do, it's water retention."

Topics of conversation drifted up and away, like bubbles. Someone asked the old woman for her milk jelly recipe, and she responded by urging her to have another one.

The hairdresser swept silently, then went to set the empty wheelie chairs in line, pausing behind each one and looking straight into the mirror, as if her gaze were a measuring tape, helping her ensure that they were even. She'd dropped out of the conversation, and her mood seemed to have darkened. Business couldn't have been going well, seeing as no one else was there for a haircut. It looked like my mother would be her last customer of the morning: four wheelie chairs remained empty. It was also possible that she had just tuned out and couldn't follow what the women were saying. That happened to me sometimes. I'd get tired and suddenly wouldn't understand a thing.

Whatever the reason, she was mute. Not even half a sentence of Indonesian-accented Malay passed her lips. She seemed to vanish into the walls; the air had no space left for her voice.

Ten minutes passed. "I've still got twenty minutes!" said my mother. "Where's she gone?"

She wasn't there. Not just mute and camouflaged; she had actually left the room. I hadn't noticed when she disappeared, but I did suddenly start noticing things that I'd previously overlooked. I saw in the mirror that there was a light hanging down from the ceiling, with butterflies fluttering against its shade, attracted by the glow. Until that moment, I hadn't even been aware of its existence. It cast a circle of light and a circle of shadow onto the floor. I was certain it hadn't been on before—I must have noticed it because someone had switched it on.

Another turn in conversation. A return to the original topic.

"That's what it's like in Ah O's house now. You know, 'we'll keep on living together but you pretend not to see me, and I'll pretend not to see you.' If something goes missing, act like you don't know who took it; if the window's broken, act like you don't know who did it. If someone empties out all the drawers, slashes all the clothes, and the chicken soup ends up as dish-soap soup—well, the house must be haunted."

"You see," said my mother, "even in that situation, life goes on."

The light above her head flickered off and on. The butterflies on the shade kept turning black. I imagined a naughty child hiding in the corner, playing with the switch.

I knew this Ah O they were talking about. He was the short man who ran the motorcycle garage near our house. People said he was too stupid to finish primary school. That he couldn't even write his own name. But if someone made a joke about how dumb his first wife was, he'd sigh, then laugh, then say, "You're right, she's totally useless, she doesn't get this is how it works. I feed her and I clothe her and she just stays at home picking fights with me. I never even say anything back. So useless. She just can't let it go."

"Ah O's kind of stupid, isn't he?"

"His mom really likes the mistress he brought home."

"She goes around telling everyone how hard-working this new woman is, but her daughter-in-law makes such a fuss. Apparently the daughter-in-law never stops yelling, and her son never has a bad word to say back."

"What? Come on, how could his mom not be disgusted by the whole situation?"

"That's just how it works!"

The world is such a strange place. This disgusting pattern just keeps on repeating. I felt myself getting angry—of course the one with all the power didn't need to argue! When you're the one with the torturous monologue droning through your head all day and night, of course you need to shout. You have to get it out. Men don't hear that voice. They keep going just as they please, not hearing anything at all.

"Here, have some water."

The old woman handed us each a cup of mineral water. We pierced the plastic film over the top with our straws and fell silent to sip it.

More time passed, and the hairdresser reappeared. She had changed into an outfit with a maroon sequinned jacket and reapplied her lipstick, as if on her way out somewhere.

"It's been half an hour," my mother reminded her.

"You're right," she said. "You should be about done."

She went to stand behind my mother and carefully began unraveling her hair from the curlers. It hung limply down her neck. I had a clear view from where I was sitting, and could sense the hairdresser's panic. A hair clip clattered into the dish on top of the cart.

The other women must have noticed too, but no one made any comment. If there was no way it could be covered up, then they would say something. From the back, my mother's hair was obviously ruined, but it wasn't so apparent from the front. I felt a stab of sympathy, but thought that if I kept quiet the hairdresser might be able to fix it. She had better try, before she headed out anywhere.

She wasn't smiling, presumably because she was worried. Her hands were working at lightning speed, like a student scrambling to finish an exam paper. Within about ten minutes, she had replaced all the curlers and slathered on an even thicker layer of lotion. She wrapped the big white towel back around my mother's head.

"So I have to wait longer?" asked my mother.

"Another half an hour should do it," mumbled the hairdresser. She looked exhausted. She was still young, but I had the feeling that those shadows on her face never went away.

"Curly hair suits you," one of the women said to my mother.

My mother rested her eyes. Or maybe she was genuinely trying to sleep. I was cold and hungry, and it struck me that the hairdresser probably was too. We all were. It wasn't easy money, this hairdressing business. Streaks of shadow danced across the window, some dark, some lighter, creating a kind of optical illusion, making me feel like I was standing outside, looking in on someone's life. Sometimes, the radio added to the confusion. I couldn't tell whether the wail of a siren was from an ambulance or a police car, and whether it was coming from the radio drama or out in the street. Couldn't tell at all.

The radio drama ended and a jingle bounced through the air. A presenter cheerfully announced, "Dear listeners, it is now thirty minutes past twelve." One by one, the women got up and left, saying they had to make lunch.

The old woman emerged from the kitchen.

"We've got nothing to eat," she said to the hairdresser.

The hairdresser opened a drawer and rummaged around. The old woman, my mother, and I watched as she closed it and anxiously opened another, and then another. Eventually, she gave up.

"I'm going to pick up the boy, so I'll buy something on

the way. I'll be back soon."

She picked up her handbag and rushed out. The three of us stood at the door like we owned the place, watching her hop onto her red Kancil scooter. She was wearing a pair of silver stilettos but moved as fast as someone fleeing a haunted house. Or maybe that was just how it seemed to me—after all, this was the second time she'd vanished right before our eyes. The scooter bounded off like a deer released from a cage.

Time, time. Time is hair. Light and mirrors. Dozing and nodding off. The sticky weight of the afternoon, the grumble of the radio.

"I've lost track," said my mother. "How long has it been now?"

"I don't know."

"She's still not back. Didn't she leave just after twelve? I thought the primary schools let out at half past one."

"I don't know. Maybe the school's far away, or she stopped off to do some shopping first."

"But how long before she comes back? Aren't you hungry?"

"No, I'm fine."

"What're you looking at?"

"Money," I said, offhandedly. I was examining the table. Rich people seem to enjoy this thing of collecting low-denomination bills and using them as decoration. There were dozens of currencies from all over South East Asia—one ringgit, five pesos, three hundred baht, five hundred thousand rupiah. Heads of state, founding fathers, and other historical personages were pressed flat and harmless beneath the glass, covering the whole of the tabletop, their faces frozen in eternal, stately smiles. Their eyes looked off to unknown places far beyond the salon walls.

My mother glanced at the table. "It's cold in here," she said, hunching her shoulders. "Aren't you cold? Much more of this and I'll freeze to death. I'm going to get some sun."

With the white towel still wrapped around her head, she opened the door and stepped outside.

When the old woman reemerged from the kitchen, we were the only two left. She told me that her son had collected the notes on the table.

"He traveled all over the place. They're from when he went abroad on business."

"What does he do now?"

She turned her stout little body to face me. There was shock in her filmy eyes, but also something else that I couldn't quite place.

"You didn't hear? You really are out of the loop, aren't you." Her eyes moistened. "He died in a car crash. He was drunk and drove into a tree."

I didn't know what to say.

"You see this house? Bought with the insurance payout. Belongs to my daughter-in-law and grandson."

"Your daughter-in-law ... ?"

"The woman who was just doing your ma's hair." She lowered her voice. "She was my son's mistress."

I could tell that I didn't need to ask any more questions, just listen. I pretended not to be too curious. Maybe she just wanted to talk about her son. That's what mothers do:

pull old tales from inside their rib cages and tell them to strangers. As if all it would take is one willing listener to bring a dead person back to life.

"He went to Indonesia on business and brought her back with him. He had a wife, but she was in Singapore and never knew anything about it. Then when he died, she came rushing up here. As soon as she realized the situation, she started screaming and yelling and kicking up such a fuss. It was terrible! Fifty years old and throwing tantrums like that, I'd never seen anything like it. No one could reason with her."

She paused for a moment, blinking furiously, trying to hold back her tears.

"We all told her to forget it. What good would it do? He was dead. My son was so good to his mistress," she continued. "He really loved her."

So the spacious, comfy house was a payment for the hairdresser's youth. When she had first met him, in that distant city, she must have been so young and unworldly.

The house was beautiful. In the glare of the midday sun, purple bougainvillea climbed up the pillars to the roof, as though trying to take over the building. A line of orange bird of paradise flowers was in full, spectacular bloom. A gutsy, rule-defying happiness seemed to be hiding inside the flourishing leaves and flower stalks, waiting for scissors to come and cut it off.

When we first arrived, we had rung a bell. The old woman came out to escort us along the fence at the side of the garden, then through the salon door. Few people would have noticed this tiny side door, because it was blocked by a washing line and a leafy canna lily. If you did happen to come close, it looked like a misty mirror. You would see the quiet street flowing across its vacant, reflective surface, and you might wonder what was happening inside. If the police walked past, they would see only their own uniforms and the twinkle of their badges. They wouldn't guess that on the other side of that mirror-like door was another mirror, big and wide and faced by empty chairs. Hairdressing salons always have too many chairs. The hairdresser hid her salon well. Of course, the set-up was perfectly ordinary. In residential areas, many homes have window glass like this, to protect against the sun. Inside, we only had to open the door and we could hear the hum of the funeral prayers on the next street, repeating over and over without pause. It occurred to me there might be a radio hiding beneath the bunches of flowers, there to broadcast the sound all day long.

Lake Like a Mirror

IF SHE'D SWERVED any harder, she would have crashed right into the lake. In the eerie twilight, the deer seemed to come out of nowhere, darting silently into the road. Of course she'd been startled. And for a few seconds all she'd wanted was to run—throw caution to the wind, shake off gravity, be gone.

In recent years, she'd be watching students bent over their desks, pens softly scratching, and a scene from the nature channel would float into her mind. A herd of elk in long grass, nestled meekly against one another. She had no idea how they grew or reproduced but, ever since that program, she thought of them often. Their chestnut fur and affection for each other. How they were wary by nature, and never spoke—at least not that humans could hear—and liked to chew on leaves. They probably had fleas, there was no way around that; every animal does. But, then again, maybe none of this was true. Maybe it was all wrong. It wasn't based on anything, and biology had never been her strong suit.

No one ever broke the rules. Hushed chatter rose from the desks, occasionally crescendoing into the crash of an ocean wave, or the clamor of a wet market. Sometimes a question would leave the students deathly silent. Sometimes an eager voice would pipe up and shatter it.

"I don't think things are as bad as the protagonist makes out."

"Why do you say that?"

"The narrator is so fixated on her own suffering, it's way too heavy-handed. The novel opens with 'Fear torments me, making me almost lose my mind.' Right from the start, it's just one crazy woman ranting to herself."

"But the tone is very detached. What's your basis for calling it heavy-handed?"

"I actually like the victim," someone else chimed in. "Maybe she enjoys the misery. Do you think it's easy to write from a victim's perspective?"

"It's an easy way to win sympathy from a reader."

Bursts of laughter, sighs, some students nodding, others shaking their heads.

A brief debate. Whispers over the desks from those who didn't participate. She waved her hands to quiet them down, pressing lightly on the air, as though conducting an orchestra.

"Do we have to rush to a conclusion? Are there clear answers, or could it be that the ending is left open to interpretation?"

She liked talking to them. Their voices filled the seminar room, rising and falling like bouncing cicadas.

"But is it so difficult just to say what happened? Why

does it have to be so ambiguous?" said one student.

"This is why I hate metafiction," said another, picking up her books and hugging them to her chest as she walked out. "It's too hard to understand."

Even the sighs and complaints sounded like the low moan of a plucked string.

There was a telecom tower outside the window. Through the slits in the blinds, it looked small and far away, like a tiny decorative sticker that kept sliding into her line of vision. When the pollution was bad, it was hardly visible, but in the evenings, driving home along the expressway, she could see it clearly in the distance, tip flashing boldly. An inland lighthouse, high above the sea of lights below, alone and cheerless in its corner of the night sky.

Our lives depend on it, she'd think to herself, every so often. Imagine that. Without it we'd be so much lonelier. But the tower itself didn't know. It sent out hundreds of thousands of messages, every single day, and it had no idea.

For a long time, she'd been careful to steer clear of trouble at work. She was thirty-five and had been in her position at the university for four years, but still felt like a baby just learning to crawl. The most she ever spoke was while teaching. And sometimes she wondered what those docile young elk took away from her seminars. Another day rolled past, and what had she said? Had she been careful enough? Could someone have misinterpreted her words? Had she been true to herself? She'd been running through this checklist since her very first day.

"They're very young. They may look like adults, but inside they're still children. In many ways, they don't yet know right from wrong, or understand the potential consequences of their actions. As their teachers, we have to be extremely careful what we say."

This was said with such seriousness that she almost wanted to laugh. But no one else in the room seemed to find it amusing. Several teaching contracts had expired, and would not be renewed. This was announced at the meeting. Announced, not discussed: the committee had made its decision. Very little was said. Items were read out and token comments were added, as usual. It was a routine affair, during which no one would object and nothing would change.

The colleague beside her sighed softly. She heard him shift closer. "Better not go causing problems around here," he whispered. "Don't be like them. Sued, fired… Didn't you start at the same time as her? Did you know her?"

She said that she wasn't sure. Maybe in passing.

At the front, the chair was still giving his earnest speech.

"Respect other people. Know where the lines are, and make sure you stick to them. You need to be vigilant, because your students are sensitive, and so are we. Very, very sensitive."

She flipped through the meeting notes on her lap.

A slogan from the government's public service department was printed along the bottom of the last page: "In service to our country and its people."

Her parents had also been public servants. Her mother a primary school teacher, and her father a primary school headmaster. From time to time, the same slogan had appeared in their house, emblazoned on a new mug or towel or umbrella or fountain pen or folder; souvenirs from training courses her parents had attended during the school holidays. She'd never thought much of it. The umbrellas would break, the towels would get moldy, the mugs would smash. Now, for the first time, she felt like the sentence was trapped in her chest, as hard and unyielding as a stone.

"Remember: it's your job to be more sensitive than they are."

I am very sensitive, she thought. It was a feeling like a thorn buried in her forehead, ready to work its way out through the corner of her mouth and pop the bubbles of chat and laughter that hung in the air. She carefully avoided it, wary of snags, but still felt uncertain. Most days, she parked under a shady tree; most days, she sat there in the driver's seat, staring into space. Windows rolled down and the world outside them surging like a sea. But she was inland, all was still. No waves. A light breeze blew through the parking lot, rippling the surface of the Biology department's fishpond.

She had an excellent memory. She could churn out names, dates, and author biographies without thinking, and would write them in long lines across the whiteboard. It intimidated people. Perhaps it was even too excellent a memory, because everything she heard stayed with her. It took a long time for her to let things go.

"We all have to learn to forget what isn't worth remembering," said her mother.

"All I have is a pile of things I need to remember," she replied.

She reminded her mother, who was killing a fish, that the fish was already dead; that she couldn't kill it twice.

"Don't tell me what to do," said her mother, slicing open the belly and scraping away the innards. She remembered how once, when she was little, she had asked why fish couldn't close their eyes. Her mother had said that fish saw everything, and that was why eating them made you clever.

"In the end, aren't we all just fish on someone's cutting board?"

"Go back to your books!" snapped her mother. "You must have better things to do. Make yourself useful!"

She went onto the balcony to keep her father company. He was smoking, looking out at the familiar view, and his face lit up at the sight of her. There was a Chinese primary school on the hill opposite, producing intermittent bursts of clarinet music. Today, she liked it, although her mother claimed to have heard sparrows that were more rousing. Every so often, names were called out over the speakers. "Huang Weixing, please report to the office." Or: "Ye Yunxin, Ye Yunxin, where are you?" And everyone in the surrounding area would hear these names, and know that these people were being looked for. She imagined a teacher standing before a rank of students, yelling into a megaphone. She imagined those Chinese schoolchildren lined up as straight and orderly as soldiers. A tiny Communist Party—that's what she and her classmates at the convent used to say. She didn't know any of the Chinese kids. They were just voices floating down the hill, sometimes drowned out by the shrieking of other nearby children or the sound of the television. She didn't know why she'd been so resistant to becoming a primary school teacher; it would have been much simpler than her current job. So much more relaxed.

"If they won't behave, then teach them a lesson," said her father, solemnly imparting his wisdom. "Make an example of someone. Don't be soft. Don't let them think you're a pushover."

At the dinner table, they talked about family. About her cousins, who were around her age. Which ones were doing well, which ones were wasting their lives, which ones were beyond all hope.

"She won't even see her siblings," said her mother. "Before, it was bad, but this is a whole new level. Always fighting with her bosses, can't hold down a job."

"People like that never get far," said her father. "They specialize in biting the hand that feeds them."

She hadn't seen these relatives for a very long time. When they were mentioned, she had only the faintest impression of who they were, like fragments from an old dream. Her parents acted as if surprised by her forgetfulness, mystified that she couldn't recall her childhood playmates, but she had left her Chinese primary school early; her parents had been posted somewhere else and she'd had to transfer. Then they'd sent her to an all-girls' convent for secondary school, and the three of them drifted apart from the rest of the family. She and her cousins had grown up to be very different people. Still, she struggled to imagine them as either these smug success stories or abject failures.

"How do you know all this?" she asked. "Who told you?"

"People talk."

She thought of one summer holiday when she was a child. At her grandmother's house, gathered on the shore with some of the cousins, watching her uncle plunge into the water. Into that big, deep lake. People were casting fishing nets off floating platforms, marking them out with rows of tightly bound bamboo, dividing the surface of the lake into little kingdoms. Her younger cousins said her uncle could dive and fix the nets underwater. He tied a thick rope around his waist and jumped. She went to the adults standing guard, and asked when he would come back up. They said she had to wait and see.

She crouched at the edge of the water, and a head suddenly broke the surface. Ripples erupted from the center of the lake, radiating in large, widening circles that sank into the wet mud of the shoreline. She wasn't sure which she'd seen first: the ripples or the person.

"Your uncle has incredible *stamina*," the adults said, using the English word. "Fixing the nets is no easy feat; he has to hold his breath, keep his eyes open to find the holes, and then stitch them back up. He has to make sure he has enough air for all that time."

The sun was so bright that afternoon it made her dizzy. She lost count of how many times her uncle came up for air. Each time he surfaced, he opened his mouth wide to the sky, as if trying to inhale the clouds.

She asked why they didn't just pull the nets in, and an older cousin told her it was too difficult, because they were big and heavy, with ropes and nails fixing them in place. Dragging them in would only tear more holes.

Talking too much was risky, and so she talked very little. She limited herself to explanations; the necessary clarifications. The seminar room, with her elk, was the only place where she felt calmer. She liked their energy and intelligence. Their naïveté. She liked how respectful they were. Liked that they asked questions and paid attention to her answers. They were very similar to her, she discovered: fond of leisure, averse to pressure. She felt less conflicted when she was around them.

If you asked them who they admired, they'd say Maugham, Carver, Tolkien, Harry Potter. No one mentioned Thomas Mann, Hemingway, Faulkner, or Virginia Woolf. If you asked why, they'd make faces.

"Hemingway's dialogue is all over the place and I don't understand it," they said.

"Too many new words, too many characters. The relationships are so confusing."

If she discounted the silent ones and painted each of those ringing questions, hypotheses, conclusions, and retorts a different color, the seminar room became a vivid tapestry. She was not displeased by the scene she had woven. Who knew whether she would have had the opportunity anywhere else. Sometimes she imagined they were animals calling to one another in a forest, each voice coming from its own shadowy location in the trees. She tried to coax the shyer ones. First, of course, they had to be allowed to listen quietly. But they couldn't be beautiful, if they let themselves merge into the same color as the leaves.

Sometimes the debates were so engrossing that she forgot to be cautious. Forgot how she liked to think of herself as the wind, working invisibly in the background, conducting other people's performances. The students had a variety of accents when they spoke English. Indian and Chinese were the most common, Malay the least. There were only four Malays in the group, and three of them stayed as quiet as shadows. The only one who didn't was an animated boy, slight but always stylishly dressed. On hot days, he turned up in tight-fitting shirts and Capri pants, wearing shoes with pointed toes. He gesticulated exuberantly when he spoke, making the silver bell on his charm bracelet tinkle.

He was from the Drama department.

"If this novel's adapted for the stage, I was born to play the part of the beautiful young Venetian."

Whistles, cheers, boos.

He fluffed his curls. "No one could be better suited."

"You've got black hair!" There was a flurry of laughter. "And you're already too old!"

She let him carry on. She doted on—was delighted to indulge—the students with obvious literary talent. She had the group read aloud from e. e. cummings's "Spring is like a perhaps hand."

and / without breaking anything.

They were happy, and their enthusiasm made her feel young. The boy read with such rhythm, almost as though he were singing. "I like 'i like my body,'" he said. There were still ten minutes left, so she let him read it. She didn't think too much about it. The poem was beautiful, and she couldn't resist beautiful things.

As he read the electrifying lines, she was struck by his

beauty. His eyelashes were very long, and fluttered across the pages. If the poet were alive, she thought, he couldn't fault him. Notes launched from the tip of his tongue and thrilled along her spine. In places, his voice went as taut as a violin string; in others, it spread wide as an opened letter. She didn't notice that other students were leaving the room.

That was April, and April passed quickly. Wind stirred the dead leaves, making them march across the ground like an army. Every so often, she'd feel calm and steady, like a clump of firmly rooted plants, no longer needing to worry about falling over. She weeded the garden at home, and noticed soft, new shoots pushing through the earth. The cuttings she'd planted earlier in the year had quickly shriveled, but there had been a spell of rain and they were struggling back to life. Spiders spun webs between their stalks.

The school on the hill was closed for the holidays, and the bell echoed through the empty building. Mosquitoes and flies glided across the murky surface of the pond.

She went to supervise an exam and spent the time staring out at the neatly mowed lawn. A flock of birds swooped past, close to the ground. She didn't hear a thing, but saw their black outlines slashing quick, jagged shapes through the sky, rising and falling, flapping on the wind, racing to catch insects before the rain. In the distance a row of manicured trees, and the sky like a low-hanging cloud. The light dimmed, blurring the view, streaking the lawn a dusky yellow. The windows were like paintings.

Before the students had arrived, she'd exchanged a few words with a Malay teacher. Purely out of habit, she'd found herself asking: "Where did you teach before coming here?"

The teacher had answered: "Malay College."

She'd been silent for a while, mulling over each word, as if counting grains of rice. She'd stared into the exam room, at the tables with their place numbers and the rows of empty chairs, and then couldn't help adding: "When you were there, did you teach any Chinese students?"

The Malay teacher had avoided her eyes. After careful consideration, she'd replied, "No, the students were all Malay."

She'd known perfectly well this would be the answer, and yet it shocked her. At the same time, she felt profoundly bored by this routine of asking things to which she knew the answers. Had the question bothered the woman? Perhaps she thought it was hostile, or deliberately provocative? It was impossible to tell; her reply had been perfectly measured. Her eyes gave nothing away. Tone appropriate, expression neutral. Calm as a millpond.

Then the Malay teacher had changed the subject, and started talking about the student who'd been caught cheating a few days before. He was going to be expelled, of course. There was a sad resignation to the woman's tone. She had hummed and nodded in response, none of it meaning anything. She thought of this as she continued to stare out of the windows, watching as the rain beat down and the lawn turned hazy.

The air conditioning was very cold and she'd woken up too early. She yawned.

She'd always liked the Malay term *air muka*, used to mean "facial expression," but literally meaning "surface of water." The expression on your face, giving away the emotions beneath. Although in reality, perhaps a rippled surface said more about the wind outside.

Talking. There were appropriate topics, and others it was better not to mention. Some people never seemed to waver over which was which.

Things hidden underwater should not be exposed to air. People laughed, but the loudest never laughed with their eyes. Their eyes were as guarded as nutshells, and their expressions were like caves: you knew at a glance that nothing would slip past them. But knowing was one thing. Knowing could not protect against moments of weakness. For example, forgetting what was appropriate. Forgetting to be vigilant. Because once you forgot, once you'd crossed that line, no matter how you tried to fix things, you'd never make them right again. You'd become gradually more isolated. Until now, the line had always been very clear.

She started to feel bored with herself, and bored with drawing the line.

May came, and the wind turned with the season. She had to remind herself to close the windows before she left work. One day she forgot, and arrived to find a shallow puddle of water in one corner of her office. This was how she discovered that her floor wasn't level.

Damp seeped into the plaster of the walls. The air conditioning was set too low for rainy days. She hunched her shoulders and walked into his office. He was reading a letter and looked up sternly from his desk as she entered, just as he usually did.

"Students tell me you've been promoting homosexuality in your seminars?" he said. "And that you made a Muslim student read a homosexual poem out loud?"

She would have defended herself, but then realized he must be referring to e. e. cummings, and even the thought of trying to explain made her feel so exhausted that in the end she said nothing at all.

"This is an extremely serious matter," he continued. "I've received complaints. I'm sure I don't need to spell it out for you, because you know what kind of place this is. There are people who prefer not to encounter these things. Naturally, you can teach whatever you like—and, well, I understand that literature shouldn't be confused with politics…but now we have this problem, and it's going to be tricky to explain to the higher-ups. To be frank, if it weren't for the complaint, I'd be inclined to ignore it."

She was silent.

"One of your students uploaded a video of himself online. There he is, on the internet, reading this poem of yours, making a speech about coming out of the closet. You should take a look, count up the death threats in the comments…

"Believe me, I wish they weren't taking this so seriously. I don't know what the committee will have to say about it. If they do decide to make a fuss—if they start picking through the egg yolk for bones, so to speak—they're going to want an explanation. You'll have to start thinking about what to say."

Her preferred option was to say nothing and have the issue quietly fade away. There was a stack of documents on his desk, the top one branded with an intricate seal. The stamped red wax was like an omen, but one too mysterious for her to decipher.

Outside the office, it was so intensely quiet that she felt her eardrums might burst. She went to the cafeteria, where she met the Malay teacher from the day of the exam. They waved at one another, both smiling weakly. Did this woman know? And if she did, was she the kind of person who liked to make trouble and would go spreading it around?

She was distracted all afternoon, arriving ten minutes late to her seminar, teaching half-heartedly. Her brain was like a mis-wired electric circuit. She filled in paperwork incorrectly and had to start again, and then again.

At dinnertime, the house filled with the blare of the television. Soap opera, ads, news, another soap opera. Her parents looked listlessly at the screen, looked listlessly at her. Or perhaps they were perfectly content, or mostly content; she couldn't tell. Then her father stopped watching television and insisted on talking, his eyes fixed on her, asserting his authority. She was his best audience. In these lonely, twilight years, she was the only remaining link between him and the outside world; between him and his fondly remembered days as a primary school headmaster. He didn't approve of her mother's approach to life. Her mother said people had to accept the hand they'd been dealt. That was just how things were. She'd been saying so for decades.

She helped her mother clear the plates, listening patiently to her as they washed up. Her mother's solitary life: to her, life was always someone else's story.

Everything about it: someone. else's. story.

When she was finally alone, she just sat there, loathe to move. She couldn't face getting into bed or brushing her teeth, just wanted to keep sitting. It occurred to her to look up that video online, and she started trying out keywords in her search bar. Eventually it appeared, but all she could see was the title, because the contents had been blocked.

That line: *This video is a grave threat to the safety of others. It has been removed.*

A shiver down her spine.

A week passed, then two. The shivers continued. She kept on going to and from her seminar room, still without any thought as to how she would explain herself to the committee. In any case, no one summoned her to a meeting. The matter was not mentioned. Had it passed? Been forgotten, just like that? Been hushed up? Or perhaps they'd reached their decision, and no explanations were necessary.

Then, at the end of the month, she heard the news: the committee had dropped her case. They had turned their focus on a younger, more troublesome teacher, who had given a lecture that touched on the restrictiveness of the Islamic dress code for women, reportedly claiming that it had become conflated with piety, but was actually rooted in ownership of a woman's body. This had antagonized a few Muslim students, who went to discuss it with the teacher in her office and subsequently pronounced her attitude "disrespectful of the Quran." They then wrote a letter of complaint to the head of the department, and the accusations snowballed from there. Coincidentally, the teacher's contract was just about to expire, and the department decided not to renew it.

It had been a busy day, and at the end of it she walked through the campus, following the slope, making her habitual detour via the Biology department's fishpond. June, and the flame trees were ablaze. She hadn't seen the Malay boy from the Drama department again.

Passing along a neon-lit corridor, she came to an open door and couldn't help pausing to look inside. The young teacher was in the middle of packing, the floor strewn with boxes. At the sound of footsteps, she looked up. Waved, said, "Hey."

And so she replied, still outside the door: "Hey." A twinge of guilt, because while she'd been reveling in her escape, she hadn't given much thought to the reason for it.

She hurried in, wanting to be friendly, eager to help, the packing tape pulling, ripping, sticking. The woman didn't object. Papers, books in English, books in Malay. A good number of books in Chinese, a few characters on their covers that she could still understand, although she stifled her curiosity. She packed the books into boxes. Then she came to the Quran with its foil-stamped cover, the eye of the storm, and froze. The woman took it from her and slid it nonchalantly into a box, continuing to stack reference books on top.

"Take whatever you like," she said. "No one can see us. Even if they could, it would be fine. There's no need to worry."

The blinds were open and the lights were on. The woman took a pack of cigarettes from her handbag and offered her one, but she shook her head. Holding one in her mouth, the woman bent forward, her hair almost covering her face, and lit it. Tobacco smoke filled the room, irritating her nose and making her nauseous; she imagined her lungs filling with muck.

"I'm very sorry. I heard what happened." Her words came out haltingly.

"What did you hear?"

"Well, I heard a bit," she said. "It wasn't very clear."

The woman looked at her curiously through the rising coils of smoke. Then she went to sit in her chair, kicking away a pile of magazines so that she could pull it closer to the desk.

"It went like this," she said, bending forward to open a drawer in the bottom left-hand side of her desk: she mimed taking something out and then, hugging a ball of air to her chest, sat back up and arranged it on her knees. "They said that when I bent forward, that was against the Quran. It was wrong."

"Oh, shit," she replied, not knowing what she was supposed to say. They had packed seven or eight boxes.

"We should go. This will take more than one day," said the woman, taking a final, decisive drag on her cigarette. "Although the sooner it's done, the better."

Even after the cigarette had been stubbed out and the ashtray emptied, the smell lingered and she felt it seeping into her clothes and hair.

The end of June shook in her ears.

"Where do you live?" she asked, nervously. "I can drop you. It'll be hard to find a taxi at this time of day."

The woman lived on the north side of the city, in a suburb near the national zoo. She knew the way because she'd been to the zoo before, to look at those lifeless animals in their cages. During the whole car ride, she felt her attention drawn to her left. They didn't exactly know each other, but neither were they complete strangers. Their offices were a few rooms apart and they had often passed one another in the corridor, gone to the same meetings, waited for one another to hand over their teaching groups. And now the woman was being singled out as an example. It was hard to fathom. She knew she should keep quiet, was aware the woman wasn't in the best mood, but they still had an hour to go. She started chatting about this and that, making fun of some stupid TV show, complaining about public transport being as shitty as ever. Then a press conference came on the radio and they both fell silent, listening as someone attacked the administration for being a festering pile of trash.

"What will you do next?" she asked, from the driver's seat.

Her passenger shrugged. "Don't know."

"What did they say to you?"

"They're smarter about these things now. It was all very civilized. They said my contract was up. That courses are being restructured and the faculty is moving in a new direction, so my services are no longer required. They didn't mention anything about student complaints."

"So that's how they played it. I guess you can't argue with that."

"Argue what?"

She didn't reply.

"Argue that I'm the victim here? Because that's not what I want."

Things were more complicated than that, she added. Much more complicated than that.

The after-work traffic was like a tide, car after car after car stretching along the outer ring road, all six lanes blocked like a huge outdoor parking lot. Horns blasted impatiently. The cars inched forward, lining up for the better part of an hour just to pass through the toll booth. In the shimmer of the setting sun, they were part of a sea that stretched all the way to the horizon.

"I might apply to go abroad, if I can find a course," said the woman, without much enthusiasm. "What about you? Things are fine now, I take it? You can stay."

She gave a small, hesitant nod, and then shook her head.

"I don't know, I hope so. Really hope so." Her voice was strained.

"I saw the video. It has nothing to do with you, some people just love to talk shit," said the woman. "English literature has nothing to do with it. They have nothing better to do than intimidate people, and try to make examples of them."

She listened silently, at a loss for words. She was sure that the woman was speaking the truth. But what was true had nothing whatsoever to do with what was safe. The two things were miles apart. Truth was further from safety than two islands at opposite ends of the earth.

They arrived and waved goodbye. Exhausted, with nothing left to say, she quickly drove off and headed home.

The car turned off the ring road and climbed uphill, entering the vast wooded area that spanned the north of the city. The last rays of sunlight lingered over the treetops, and the narrow road snaked through dark tree trunks and their hazy shadows. Shrubs and branches melded into walls of greenery on either side until, abruptly, they gave way to a wall of billboards. A whole row of advertising for real estate.

It was here that the animal sprang out of nowhere—an elk, or at least something a lot like an elk, appearing all of a sudden outside the window on the driver's side.

Those marvelous antlers. It raced past, the forest trailing behind. Perhaps it wasn't an elk; perhaps just an ordinary deer. She couldn't be sure because biology had never been her strong suit.

She couldn't see the whole thing, just parts of it, flashes of head and body, bobbing frantically up and down as it ran, as though being chased by a wild beast. Or as though jumping for joy, just released from a cage. For a few seconds, she completely forgot that she was driving, and couldn't tear her eyes away: such a creature, and for it to have come so near! Right outside her window, silky fur so close she could have touched it. Antlers within easy reach. These were shorter and smaller than the antlers she'd seen on television; a little like broken branches, as though battered by the elements, left hardened and gray. Its neck was long, and its eye seemed to stare straight at her from the side of its head, even while it was running away at full pelt, toward something she did not know and could not see.

Briefly, they ran together along the silent road, the shadows of the trees sheltering them like a nest. In the ink-blue twilight, it was as if she'd crossed into a dreamworld, her everyday consciousness peeled back and replaced by a new, peculiar sensitivity that surged like a wave, so powerful that she felt she might fly. Might leave the surface of the earth, be swept beyond the horizon and no longer belong to any time, or any place.

It was just a split-second thing. Then there was a giant bend and the car spun and she snapped awake, slamming on the brakes. The wheels screeched. The animal overtook the car, continuing its elegant, carefree sprint around the bend. One second and it had abandoned her, becoming a shrinking gray dot at the end of the road.

The car leaped the curb, left the road, and charged into the wasteland that surrounded the lake. It was over before she could scream.

She slowly came to her senses, and found herself still in her seat. Gingerly, she checked the rearview mirror and, seeing no cars on the road behind, began to reverse. Her back wheels jammed in a muddy ditch. No matter how the engine roared, they would only spin on the spot.

She turned off the engine. A cloud of mosquitoes flew up, and her ears flooded with an insect whine. The flickering gleam of the water. She could make out a pile of abandoned furniture. There was a sofa right at the edge of the lake—close enough that, if you sat on it, you would surely be able to touch the water with your toe. It was an enticing prospect, beckoning to her like a holiday, but as she walked closer she realized it was impossible to reach. It was surrounded by old wood and assorted junk. She examined this collection of messy, damp objects, hoping to find boards to put under her wheels.

The mosquitoes attacked her arms and legs. She

returned to the car and restarted the engine, but it was no good. She remained trapped as the sky and the lake turned completely black, desperately trying to phone for help. There was no reception; all she heard was the electronic recording from the service provider, over and over again.

She was wild with frustration. There wasn't a single streetlight.

She knew that she was some distance from the lake. But she couldn't see anything; her eyes were wide open and she couldn't see. The absolute darkness distorted her perspective. She thought of those creation myths and their revered heroes, tearing order from chaos; of their incredible courage. Their astonishment when they saw the first ray of light, and discovered they had eyes. She knew all she had to do was turn on her headlights, but couldn't decide which was safer: to alert others to her existence, or continue to hide in the dark?

She sat quietly for a moment, listening carefully. Listening to the unfamiliar noises out there in the night, the jagged harmony of the trees and insects. Confronting the pitch-black chaos. The wind gusted across the lake. She heard it blowing across her car, through the shrubs and the undergrowth, and she had the weary thought: that's how it is, that's how it is. Now rest for a while.

The Chest

AN YAH BENT DOWN to the sideboard next to the sewing machine. It was almost as old as she was, its clear plastic door speckled with brown. Dust clumped thickly over the hinges and she had to wrench to get it open. Today, she planned to clear out the junk inside. There was a wooden chest in there, once home to an old-fashioned gramophone. Until about nine years ago, black vinyl records were always spinning on the gramophone's turntable, their old tunes accompanying the steady rumble of the sewing machine pedal. But the gramophone was gone. Sold off, along with all the records, following its owner out of this world and into the past. An Yah heaved the chest toward her and saw it was filled with odds and ends from who knew when, that she couldn't remember putting there. A dusty cobweb hung off one side. At the time, she hadn't been able to bear the thought of giving it away. Now, she just wanted to be rid of it, and free the space for two big sacks of plastic slippers.

It was heavier than she'd expected. Or maybe it was just

that she was bent over, at a bad angle for pulling. Her cream slacks were covered in dusty gray fingerprints. Over the last two years, she had been increasingly lax about cleaning; she was too busy. The gaps between cabinets and the out-of-the-way corners were full of cobwebs, and a thin layer of dust covered all the goods in the shop. Customers didn't seem to care—they usually tracked in dusty, muddy footprints of their own—and it had never bothered An Yah. Dust, mud, spiders, geckos: they were part of life. Once upon a time, a large plump hand had brandished scissors, unrolled bolts of cloth across the counter, cut off lengths, rolled the remaining cloth back up, and the dust had stayed away. Now there was only her, and there was so much dust that it didn't really matter whether she cleaned or not.

In the reflection of a cabinet door, she watched Wood Lim enter the shop. He turned up every few days with a bundle of vegetables, appearing once he'd closed up his stall at the morning market. It was pure speculation on his part, because An Yah didn't recall ever having asked him to do it. But the vegetables were always fresh and he gave her a good price, so she allowed it to continue.

She called out a greeting, still tugging at the chest. It was half out, tilting toward the floor.

Usually, Wood put the vegetables on the counter, took his money, and left. But today, seeing what the situation was, he strode over to help.

"Here, let me!" He pushed aside the sewing machine, a shoe-display cabinet, and a rattan chair.

An Yah moved out of his way, leaving the box teetering over the edge of the cupboard.

"I can do it by myself!" she protested.

"Come on, this thing is heavy!"

And it was, surprisingly so. Who'd have thought that such a decrepit old sideboard could hold such a weight? The pulled-out end balanced precariously on Wood's knee. An Yah rushed to support the left-hand side, which looked on the verge of crashing to the ground. Perspiring heavily, the two of them finally managed to get the chest out and carefully set it on the floor.

"What the hell have you got in there?" muttered Wood.

She wasn't entirely sure herself. It looked like bits of leftover fabric. Denim, linen, flannel, cotton, bits of polyester. Dust flew up as soon as she touched them. Wood sneezed.

An Yah went behind the counter to fetch him his money.

"One fifty," he said.

She gave him two.

"You're pretty strong," he remarked, as he took it.

He rested for a moment in a chair behind a glass cabinet. Threads of morning sun crept through the seams of the window blinds. There was a pleasant breeze. Sparrows chirped beneath the eaves. Through the blinds, down by the river, there was a mango tree. Some flowers. Some wild vegetables.

Wood had nowhere to be. He had never known the shop's former towkay; by the time he started bringing vegetables over on his scooter, Big Man had been dead for several years. If he'd still been around, perhaps they would have chatted. An Yah was absorbed in tidying up her junk pile, and hadn't said a word. After a while, Wood spotted the lady next door out for a walk and, curious, got up and left.

The chest used to have a lid, but who knew where that had ended up. In the old days, the gramophone used to sit on top, its needle traveling inward. Even after cassette tapes took off, Big Man insisted on listening to records. He took great pleasure in the little rituals that went along with it, carefully wiping the records with a scrap of velvet, inspecting their grooves, then sliding them back into their cases. He had over a hundred of them, filling three drawers and a cupboard. An Yah remembered all his old habits. Thirty years of marriage, during which they had changed both enormously and hardly at all. The sewing machine, gramophone, bamboo blinds, sideboard, and various other furniture had been in Big Man's family since long before the two of them married. For the better part of half a century, the room had barely changed. The major transformation had happened when Big Man died and An Yah became a widow. This old place had become hers.

The chest stayed where An Yah and Wood had left it. A whole day went by and An Yah did not touch it. Customers came and went. A few curious children peered inside. Some tried to bury their faces in the old fabric scraps and were scolded by adults. Eventually, a couple of customers, looking for somewhere to sit down and try on shoes, found it was in the way and helped her push it behind a shoe rack. Then they carried over a low stool and used the chest as a back rest. No one seemed to mind the dirt.

"Towkay, I didn't bring enough money. I've only got fifteen."

An Yah looked at the shoe box and saw she had written "Same Fit" on it. "Same Fit" meant this pair had cost twelve ringgit. Same, fit, fancy, flat, good, big, small, long, pair, tie. Ten family code words, telling her the trade price. This code had been passed down from her parents-in-law, who had taught it to Big Man, who had taught it to her and the children. Outsiders would never be able to crack it. Even within the family, she was the only one who could still decipher it; her children and Big Man's younger brothers had long since forgotten.

"Eh, but that leaves nothing for me. Come back with enough money next time."

"Can I owe you?"

An Yah nodded reluctantly. "But remember to pay it."

She turned and made a note on the whiteboard behind the counter.

"And don't go around telling everyone."

The customer grinned, pausing on the way out to ask, "What's cooking back there? Smells good."

"Nothing," said An Yah.

She hadn't cooked at lunchtime since her children left home. She needed to keep her eyes on the shop. Big Man used to stay in the front while she cooked in the back, taking her time, pans wheezing and clattering, filling the shop with the rich fragrance of stir-fried scallions and garlic. But now the most practical course of action was to get food delivered. For fifty-five ringgit a month, a lunchbox of one meat and two vegetable dishes was dropped at her door daily, meaning she could eat in between customers. When one walked in, she closed the container and slid it under a newspaper. Usually, she ate half and saved the rest for dinner. If she got too hungry and finished it all, then in the evening she'd boil Wood's vegetables and eat them with rice.

The chest had given off an odd, musty smell, like rusting nails after a rainstorm. But after sitting with it for a while, she found it started to smell cleaner and sweeter, like hay. The scent drifted into the center of the room, where she noticed that some customers seemed hungrily drawn to it; unconsciously, they'd move closer to the box and inhale deeply. Others remained oblivious, their body odor overpowering enough to mask it.

A boy came in to buy a loose cigarette. He borrowed a lighter and exhaled a heady cloud of Marlboro, which instantly curled around the shop. Then he asked for some shoelaces, a pair of socks, and some wrapping paper, in quick succession. As An Yah packed up the items, she saw him lean back against the chest and casually flick his cigarette butt onto the floor.

She watched numbly, still unsure what to do about the chest. I should just get rid of it, she thought. But when there was finally a lull in customers, she felt she should seize the chance to go to the toilet.

It was one of the difficulties of running the shop by herself: she often had to ignore the urge for hours at a time. To lessen the need, she drank little water, which in turn made her constipated. Her daughter warned her that if she didn't drink enough, she'd get kidney stones. But every time she left the shop and went into the back for a glass of water, or to turn on the lights, or the fan, she felt uneasy, worried that a thief would take advantage of her absence. Once, her daughter had left her phone beside the shop's ancestral shrine, and when she'd gone to pick it up a little while later, it had vanished.

When An Yah came back from the bathroom, she noticed the hay scent again, coiled about the room like a snake. She sat on the little stool, leaning back against the chest. This close, the smell was intense. She inhaled deeply, filling her chest with it, and felt herself relax. She sighed, and then sighed again, and had the vague impression of Big Man wavering before her, although his face was hazy. He said something but she didn't catch it. It made her suddenly anxious and she wanted to say, *Speak up! You're all fuzzy*. But the words lodged in her throat.

"Hey, towkay!" called a Malay kid, summoning her back to the present.

At six o'clock that evening, she heaved over the two heavy wooden door panels that stood leaning against the wall. No one else had doors like this anymore; they'd all upgraded to lightweight aluminium roller shutters, and installed iron grates over their windows. She would have liked to replace her panels with iron grates—then she could just pull them closed and go to the toilet, take a nap, or have a shower, without having to worry. But the wooden doors had been there since her in-laws first started the shop. People often remarked that they were the oldest of all the old curios in town. She had a photo of her in-laws, in which her mother-in-law was barely twenty and dressed in a traditional Chinese jacket and pant suit, while her father-in-law stood stiffly beside her in a neat Western-style one (it was hard to imagine that such a well-turned-out young man would go on to become such a slave to his opium pipe). In the background, embedded sturdily in their frame, were the wooden doors. By the looks of things, they had been there much longer than the couple: in the year after the in-laws had arrived from China, while they were moving between relatives' houses, trying to find their feet, the doors would have already been in place.

An Yah stood outside and carefully slotted the door panels into the notches in the doorstep. When she had finished, she shook out her arms, feeling as though she could hardly lift them. Even her mother-in-law, the shop's original and longest-serving resident, had given up on them eventually. Yet every morning when she opened up the shop, An Yah lifted the panels out of their slots and carried them over to lean against the wall. Then, at closing time, she carried them back again. Since Big Man had been gone she'd had to do it all by herself. The panels were thick and solid and who knew how heavy. Her daughters struggled to manage just one.

I should tidy up, thought An Yah, worrying that there would be nowhere for her second daughter to sit when she arrived. But she was so tired. She sank into a chair on the walkway outside and watched the sun set through the trees opposite the door, its light marching slowly along the gravel road. A whole day of selling things, doing the inventory, restocking, checking the accounts. It was exhausting. The children had grown up and moved out, so she could be a little more relaxed about finances, and since Big Man had passed away she'd been expanding the stock. Now, merchandise flooded from the shop all the way to the little kitchen at the back, and had taken possession of the sofa and armchairs that no one ever sat on anyway. Goods occupied almost all available space, leaving only a tiny patch of floor for her to sweep every day. The rest she left to the rats and the cockroaches.

Her second daughter pulled up outside the shop. She parked her white car in the street and stepped out holding an assortment of grocery bags.

"I bought you horseshoe biscuits," she announced.

She pushed the panels open and sneezed as soon as she came inside. "What's that smell?" she asked, setting down the bags. With the doors closed, the hay scent had intensified. Even though she didn't have a particularly sensitive nose, she was instantly guided to the source and cried out in surprise: "When did this turn up? Didn't you throw it out ages ago?"

An Yah didn't hear her. She had gone into the kitchen to prepare dinner. Her daughter drew a bucket of water from the tap and started wiping down surfaces in the shop. When An Yah came out to tell her the food was ready, the shop floor was soaking wet. Her daughter was kneeling in front of the chest, digging out dark clumps from the bottom and sniffing them.

"What are they?" she asked, dubiously.

An Yah stared for a while. "Who knows."

"I didn't think we still had any of these chests. It's in quite good condition…"

"Have it, if you want," said An Yah.

Her daughter was still puzzled. "But didn't you sell it

to that Indian junk collector?"

An Yah couldn't remember what she might have sold or thrown out. She was old, she forgot a lot of things. It was only natural. But what she said was, "You're never home, what would you know?"

They ate in near silence, the only sound coming from a soap playing on the television. An Yah had cooked the vegetables from Wood's delivery that morning. Carrots and broccoli. She had even cut the carrots into little flowers. Every so often, she or her daughter glanced at the television. The commercials came on. They chatted half-heartedly, in an uneven back-and-forth. An Yah found her daughter's questions tedious. Her daughter felt the same way about hers.

"You don't eat much," said her daughter.

"I'm old," she replied.

A little later, An Yah asked, "So your work's all in English?"

"Yeah," said her daughter.

"How do you say 'old'?"

"*Ohh—*"

"*Ouuuuu—er—*!" An Yah drew out the sound. Her daughter continued to eat and glance at the television.

"Sounds like an old dog," said An Yah.

That night, she tossed and turned, listening to the steady breathing of her daughter. At three in the morning, she got up to go to the bathroom and heard a noise coming from the shop. It sounded like a rat gnawing on something. Worried it might be gnawing on her stock, she took a flashlight and went to investigate.

It was too dark to see. The scent clung to the tepid

air—could it be attracting the rodents? The flashlight was dim. She skimmed the beam over the counter, then a line of shoes and plastic sandals, a pile of boxes. Nothing unusual, until it landed on the chest. Her mind drifted backward, as if fast asleep, sifting through yesterday, the day before, and she found herself wondering: How is this thing still here? The beam continued to rove the room, briefly illuminating the door. It was tightly closed. The yellow circle of light flitted across the floor at the front, showing up the crack in the cement, full of grime that sweeping couldn't touch. Little children liked to poke their fingers inside, as though hoping to unearth treasure. Something caught in her nose. She sniffed, and there was the serpentine trail of the scent again. All of a sudden, she understood her daughter's shock at seeing the chest: it was true, she had thrown it out. She remembered now. She shivered and turned back into the bedroom, where she lay down and pulled up her quilt.

She still couldn't sleep. Sadness crept through her body and she started to cry. I don't want to be alone, she thought, over and over again. Life keeps on going but there's no joy anymore. The floorboards felt very cold. She knew there would be no response to her crying. She refused to move in with her daughters and their husbands. Their marriages had enough problems without her adding to them. But the loneliness was terrifying. In the darkness of the universe, her fate had been decided. She felt her strength wither. Life was an infinite sea of bitterness. She thought: If I fall asleep and never wake up, that's fine by me. Dawn was approaching by the time she finally drifted off.

She woke to her daughter's yelling. The room was filled with brilliant sunshine. She scrambled up, alarmed by the noise, and hurried downstairs, where she picked her way around the scattered goods and arrived at the doors. Her daughter had pushed them open and was standing outside, staring in horror at the metal air vent that ran along the top of the shopfront. Someone had cut a large hole.

She told her daughter about the disturbance in the night. Evidently, the culprit had been scared off his night-time activities by her flashlight.

"Something could have happened," said her daughter.

They called the police, but since there was no real damage, the police were unconcerned.

"No harm done," said one officer, a tall man with a booming voice. "Nothing taken, no one hurt. Nothing for us to do here."

The two officers who had responded to the call were very big, and their presence made the shop feel very small. With the chest there, space was even more restricted. One of them stood on the doorstep, a cigarette dangling from his mouth, exhaling clouds of smoke into the shop. His eyes were fixed on one, lonely flip-flop that had fallen inside the chest. Neither policeman was in uniform; they wore their own checked cotton shirts, and somehow this relaxed attire made them seem even taller and sturdier. An Yah looked toward the door and saw them silhouetted against the light outside, casting enormous shadows across the floor, shrugging their hulking, gorilla-like shoulders.

She was unhappy with their comments, but said nothing.

"You've been very lucky," said the one without a cigarette.

"No damage. He didn't get inside. In the kampung down the road, thieves will even steal the water meter from your outside tap! Those things are worth seventy, eighty bucks. They've taken them from so many houses, we can't keep up. Best not to keep valuables outside."

The two of them paced back and forth in front of the door and then went to inspect the hole. The smoker dropped his butt on the floor and ground it out with his foot. He stared at the hole for quite some time, hands on hips, then scratched his chin and muttered, "Huh. Impressive. That metal is thick."

Then he sniffed. "What's that smell?" he asked, turning to face An Yah.

The other one had noticed it too, and held his nose raised like a dog's. They came inside, sniffing enthusiastically until a breeze blew through the shop and the trail went cold.

"What is it?" they asked one another.

An Yah felt her irritation rise. They were useless. She regretted having called them. These bastards were only good for stirring up trouble, not for resolving anything. She shouldn't have stayed up all night fretting over nothing; it had clouded her judgment. She had no idea how to reply to their question, but her daughter stepped in: "Our fridge is broken."

The policeman seemed doubtful. "Is that so?"

Without waiting for a reply, he marched into the kitchen. An Yah's pulse quickened. She couldn't take her eyes off the chest. She knew she shouldn't look at it, but the more she told herself that, the less power she had to look away. The policeman came back out, shaking his head at An Yah, chuckling.

"Towkay, your fridge isn't cold. Much longer and your vegetables will be ruined."

She instantly relaxed, nodding obediently. For a few weekends in a row, none of her children had come over and she hadn't bothered to cook. With every delivery from Wood, the contents of the fridge had grown, until she'd completely lost track. It was crammed with shriveled produce. Tomatoes, radishes, cabbage, old tofu.

"How about I give you some?" she said.

Satisfied that they'd done their job, the policemen strolled out of the shop. As they left, one turned to An Yah.

"You know," he said, "this kind of thing isn't really a police matter. Next time, take a look around yourself. If there's less than five hundred ringgit's worth of damage, best to let it be."

An Yah watched them cross the road and disappear down a side street. Then she and her daughter set about moving the chest into the kitchen. It wasn't an easy process: An Yah had to clear away piles of merchandise, and then the two of them had to half-drag, half-carry the chest along the newly cleared route.

"Last night I suddenly remembered why it's so heavy," said An Yah. "This isn't Dad's gramophone chest, it belonged to your granny."

"To Ah Nei? You mean we had two?" Her daughter was surprised. She clasped her hands to her face and sighed with relief. "I thought you had thrown it away and then regretted it, and secretly gone to get it back."

"Why would I do that? There's too much stuff here as it is."

"That's what you're like, though! You never throw anything away. You live in a glorified trash heap!"

"Nonsense." An Yah was getting angry. "Now you're just nagging."

"The whole house is full of junk!"

"If you don't like it, don't come over!"

Her daughter did not reply.

The wood of the chest was in perfect condition, not rotten at all.

"If Ah Nei were here, she'd hack it up for firewood…"

"Things like this are always turning up in this house…" said her daughter.

The house had been home to so many dead people.

An Yah knocked on the bottom layer of wood inside the chest. It sounded hollow. The nails were firmly in place. She hunted around the kitchen for a claw hammer to pry them out, pushing aside towels and cleaning rags drying on a line. When she opened the drawers, cockroaches and geckos scurried out in all directions.

Other people's kitchens weren't so stuffed with cupboards. Big Man's uncles had made these ones. Aside from the big display cabinets, all the furniture in the shop was at least fifty or sixty years old. The little stools, the long sideboard used for ironing, the ancestral shrine. The wood was old and hard, exceptionally sturdy, varnished to a high shine, all as heavy to lug around as those doors she carried in and out, every morning and evening.

"I sold one off, this one was probably under Ah Nei's bed or something. How it got out here, I have no idea. I was confused. I forgot which one it was. I just assumed it was the one your dad kept his gramophone in."

Finally, she found an ax in the back of a drawer.

"Stand back," she warned her daughter.

And she started hacking the chest apart.

Summer Tornado

THE FERRIS WHEEL PAUSED in its rotation for one, electrifying minute, and Su Qin's basket was right at the top.
Sunday afternoon, dazzling sunlight, glittering halos all
across the park. Viewed from the summit of that enormous,
steel-boned loop, the carnival below was a heady whirlpool
of swirling, billowing colors, spinning too fast for her to
focus. Her body felt as if it were about to break apart and
scatter, like a sheet of paper blowing through a metal grate,
ready to be snatched by the wind. The wheel was hardly
a rollercoaster or a flying saucer ride, but still, icy terror
poured down from the crown of her head. It was as if all
that empty air had tied her up and now held her teetering
over the sheer drop, and if she could just look up toward the
sky there'd be something there to save her, but no matter
what she tried, she couldn't lift her head to see it.

"Today, there will be, changes, I, we, we must—"
    The sentence cut off there. The wheels of the cassette

tape kept turning, click-click, like a rolling skull, click-click, its vacant eyes seeking the spinning world outside. Su Qin wanted to say something else but all she had to offer was blankness. She couldn't turn it into voice. When she was left alone, when she felt abandoned or as if she needed to take charge, she would tell herself stories. But now, trying to talk into the microphone, she was ridiculous. She tried to force out a sound: *Oh*—

Her own voice, recorded, played back. She'd never understood why people seemed to resist her, until she heard herself through the headphones. Her voice was tight and anxious, as if a snake were hiding inside it, hissing between the sentences.

She had attempted to change her accent but couldn't, and on top of that a certain stubborn timbre remained, like scales sticking to the ends of her words. She drew out her *I* and listened as it slowly morphed into an *O*. The tape deck's batteries were running down and the stretched syllable sounded like an animal howling in a cave. During the parts of the tape where she hadn't recorded yet, the machine rustled quietly.

Her first ten years abroad she'd been hopeful. She'd gone to work in Singapore after graduation and, a few years later, followed a man to Taipei to get married. Back then, she had believed that if you didn't take risks things would always stay the same. Nothing good would ever happen. Wonderful things awaited you, as long as you were careful enough; as long as you held the tray steady and didn't let them slide off and smash.

She had worn her orange flip-flops to the park. A sunny orange, allowing her to stride out with confidence. This would be a fresh start. They would forget the past. Old misunderstandings were just lingering shadows, that was all, and they would disperse soon enough.

For the past few days, she had been plagued by a nagging sense that everything was turning to dust, a thought that ticked like a clock inside her body. It was especially acute at night, just before she fell asleep, when the wind whistled past her twelfth-floor windows. From that height, nighttime Taipei lay beneath her like a flashing neon mask, inviting her to leap down and grab it. But a voice in her head would rise to soothe the sleep-crazed ramblings. It was strong and assured, a lifeline thrown down to someone drowning in a swamp. It came from so high up that she couldn't see the source, dangling there to remind her: *You still haven't…* Still hadn't what? There were many things she "still hadn't." *But*, it seemed to say, *if you look on helplessly as the rope vanishes from your hands, of course you'll continue to drown—and then what?*

Two years of feuding, and all the things they'd kept hidden had been dragged into the light. But today would not be just another outing. She was not going to keep muddling along like this. She was going to make an important decision, based on an important test.

Her body was starting to sag and she felt self-conscious in her swimsuit, so she pulled a shirt out of her backpack before leaving the basket. Then she stepped out and rejoined the clamor. Watery gurgles clashed against the giant metal spokes and technicolored sunlight magnified inside splashes from the pool. Shouts and laughter clung to the summertime humidity and swelled through the park. The dripping-wet crowd jostled and pushed. Everyone was grinning, barely able to see through the water streaming from their eyes.

She had not been in the water yet. She was wearing a straw hat. Brilliant sun scattered across every living creature. There were the people she had been waiting for; she followed them. There was that voice she heard every day, hanging in the air in front of her feet. That tone which said, *We're completely at ease. We accept each other as we are, no need to change.* Now they were stepping across the sand and hurling themselves into the water, there they went: a husband, a son, a daughter. Inexplicably wild with delight, racing into the man-made waves. She found herself wading in after them. Suddenly, she was part of a big group of strangers, all encased in colorful inner tubes, holding their breath as they awaited the thrill of the next big wave. Her body felt weightless, too insubstantial to capsize, but the collective pretense was that the waves might drown them. It's fine, she thought. With this many people, we're more likely to be crushed to death.

She saw the husband (or father) half-floating, half-kneeling in between the two children. His extended arms were glaringly white, each one clutching a tube attached to a child. The three of them were chained together by those sturdy arms, holding them steady against the waves. A wave broke and they were giddy with laughter, splurting water out of their throats and noses. The man relaxed his grip for a moment, as he moved to wipe a face. Then all their faces creased, their three pairs of eyes angling down at the corners as they smiled. They were so alike.

Su Qin decided to play a silent game. To shut up, say nothing. She decided to quietly vacate her position, leaving them to their happy, motherless scene.

"Having fun?" A nod.

"Time to get out?" A shake of a head.

The man held the children close, nervously reminding them to hold tight to their inner tubes. They were having a wonderful time. Their father's hair was thinning on top, but his shoulders were broad. He looked reliable.

Su Qin thought of her own mother. Bestower of so many strengths and so many flaws. She remembered that hug, her mother's mouth pressed to her ear, breath hot on her neck, as if trying to blow life into a stubborn clay doll. "Now listen to me, wherever you end up, make sure you get married and have children. You hear? Don't let yourself grow into a lonely old woman."

Su Qin felt the tears come, right there in the pool.

Her mother had found a hundred ways to tell her the same thing. She had repeated it so many times that Su Qin came to think of it as her mother's golden rule. It seemed the thing she most wanted to say, in all her life.

There were words trapped in Su Qin's gut. Words that she desperately wanted to say but couldn't seem to get out. It was never the right moment, and so they had stayed inside her for years, wearing each other down. Maybe they were pointless and she didn't really mean them. She had no way of knowing which ones were worth saying. Maybe in the moment before she died, she would suddenly know, and as soon as she spoke them out loud everything would be OK. But then again, what if it meant that she would go her whole life without ever knowing? Then what?

One of the best things about the amusement park was that it was like a big party where you barely needed to talk. You could prove yourself by how enthusiastically you had fun. How wildly you laughed, shrieked, ran away in terror. You carried your inner tube, rushed from here to there, slid from high to low, charged from low to high. As the sun burned into her skin, Su Qin discovered the amusement park had a face other places didn't show. Every place has expressions particular to itself, like the ones you encounter inside a train car, or an elevator. The amusement park's face was permanently convulsed with gaiety. An intense, deathly gaiety that radiated from bodies in beams, like sunlight, gradually cooking every bodily fiber until your whole being was scalding hot and you had no choice but to run around in panic.

Tired of the artificial waves, the girl came back across the sand, picking her way in quick little steps. Now the three of them were running somewhere else. In all this joyful coming and going, they would never have believed her if she'd told them that time was fleeting, and they had only a few years left to be together like this. Imagining herself an invisible mother, ignored by her family, Su Qin silently followed, watching their shadows bounce beneath the sun.

They came to a big castle and the children launched into climbing up its slides and stairs, riding the water flumes into the pool. Along with other park children, they splashed down and climbed back up while waves crashed in and knocked them over, showing off to the assembled parents how quick and clever they were, how nothing could stand in their way.

They ran to the beach to play volleyball. Then, somewhere else again, the three of them sat in a rubber dinghy, shrieking as it spun round and round in a huge inflatable bowl. Ten minutes later, Su Qin watched as they were discharged into a small artificial river, weak with exhaustion.

"Shall we go home now?"

"No, no! We haven't done that one! Let's go on that one!"

"My God." The father looked at the train, currently climbing leisurely up its tracks, soon to come swooping down at breakneck speed, almost nothing standing between its passengers and the air. "Am I allowed to say no? Will you come?"

She did not reply right away. She lifted her camera and aimed it at them, adjusting the lens to bring his face closer, magnifying it and then pushing it away, making it shrink again. She wanted his face to tell her whether it was a genuine plea, or just asked for the sake of asking. But all she saw was exhaustion. Flat, lifeless eyes that were entirely devoid of warmth, staring stonily into the lens. She hoped it was from all the playing, not because of the last few years. On the camera screen, the three of them were standing side by side, hemmed in by colorful balloons, cartoons, giant metal skeletons, and plastic toys, with almost no space left for anything else.

Now they were in a long line, waiting to board the roller-coaster. Su Qin was very close to them; any bystander would naturally assume that she was the real mother of the family. The father reached out as though to touch her shoulder, but at the last minute his hand settled on his daughter's soft hair. He hugged her to him and planted a kiss on her forehead. He pulled a face, causing his sunglasses to slip down his nose, but the girl didn't find it funny. She scowled. In the background, chatter swelled like a sponge, pressing itself so tightly around them that no joy could permeate.

At regular intervals, there came a deafening cheer from the descending ride. As it swept over their heads, Su Qin felt her scalp go cold, as though scraped by a razor. She had agreed to come because of that ghostly voice; because otherwise the wind that blew past the apartment at night would suck her in like a whirlpool and spit her out below.

Of course I'll do it, she thought, confused. Even if it only numbs me for a while, at least that's something.

She observed the boy, who was standing in front of her, calmly blowing bubbles. She guessed he must be nervous, but he hid it well; if he was shaking, she couldn't see it. His face was blank and his eyes were fixed serenely on the tip of his straw as it sprouted iridescent orbs. They rose into the sky, getting bigger, higher, even bigger, even higher, and then they popped. That was how the carnival felt too. As if it might suddenly stop.

She heard a girl behind her tell her mother that she needed to pee. Without hesitating, her mother led her away from the line. They didn't come back.

You need to find a way to talk to him, she thought.

Once he starts talking, the line will go faster. Except you know you can't do it, because the second you open your mouth, there come the tears.

She told herself it was all a dream. Now, all those impossible discussions would be possible. All those things she never thought could happen, would happen.

"Are you OK?" The boy had turned around to look at her.

"Yes," she smiled. "Of course."

The silent game was over. But this time, one of them had spoken first. In spite of her tight voice, in spite of her strange accent, they had had to open their mouths and speak to her. She ruffled the boy's hair and he didn't resist. In all this time, he had yet to address her directly. What was he supposed to call her—Aunty? Stepmom?

"You don't have to come," he said. "If you're scared."

"I'm not scared."

"My mom would be scared. Last time she waited for us at the exit."

This was news to Su Qin. Had they always been similar, she and this woman? Or had she, by stepping in as a replacement, grown to become like her?

"I'm not that scared."

"But if the train falls off…"

She tried to reassure him. She didn't understand this hellish merriment at all; tear down the flimsy fun houses, and all you would be left with was sand. But she was willing to convince him of what she wanted to believe herself.

"It won't fall off, not in a hundred years."

She would never get on this ride again. Being flipped over and suspended upside down made her feel like a trash-can, upended and shaken vigorously. Her body felt tightly absorbed into the seat but something inside it seemed about to fly out, as if a piece of her soul were being claimed by the wind.

She screamed uncontrollably along with everyone else, although she didn't know whether to scream "waa" or "yaa" and couldn't hear what the others were doing. An intense, almost painful gaiety seized her body, pressing against her heart like a swollen sponge.

Maybe this was all a dream. Maybe she'd passed out. A cloud of white fog rose up from beneath her nose, gradually expanding, swelling until it completely covered her eyes. For a moment, she was blinded, no longer able to see the blur of scenery racing past her. All she saw was slick, dense, pristine white. A nauseating blankness. A clamminess. There was nothing there, but nothing could get through it. It squatted on her head, smearing itself against her face. She couldn't struggle against it; it was as if she were a rigid corpse wrapped inside milk-white wax. All she could do was scream, angrily emptying the air from her lungs, until something else came creeping along her throat and she felt herself start to vomit.

The sheet of white over her eyes and nose gradually lightened, shrank, pulled away from her face. It became weightless, took on a kind of glossy curve. She could clearly see an enormous white *O* emerging from her open mouth.

Two *O*s. Three. She lost count. They floated up one after the other into the boundless blue of the sky.

No one saw, she thought. She had vomited white balloons.

The father was sitting in front of her, of course he hadn't seen. The boy was sitting next to her, but she didn't know if his eyes had been open. He hadn't stopped screaming for the whole ride. Oh, he definitely hadn't seen: afterward he said to her, "You weren't sick."

He looked confused. She could read the sentence that was hiding inside his chest: You see, you're not like us.

As soon as they were off the ride, the three of them opened paper bags and violently threw up. Su Qin thought back to that morning, when they'd ordered hamburgers, rice au gratin, ham and chicken cutlets, fries, icy soda. She hadn't tried to stop them.

They kept their heads lowered, convulsing in the same way, at the same tempo. They were so alike, from how they kneaded their stomachs to their dazed expressions as they tried to calm their breathing. She handed out tissues. When she collected their bags of vomit, she felt a wave of nausea.

It wasn't just because they were another woman's children. Even if she had given birth to them herself, they could still have grown up to be more like their father. But if they could become his children, maybe they could become her children, if she fought for it. If, if. If she loved them until she died. Maybe then they would have to talk to her, despite her obvious accent, and slowly, eventually, bit by bit, maybe they would love her back.

But they would still leave her. When she died, she would be alone, she would die a lonely old woman.

The afternoon was never-ending. She felt like she'd been stewing in it for days. On the other side of the park, they walked by a big heart-shaped spinning teacup.

"How about another ride?"

The children looked at her in alarm.

Su Qin went in first. She sat down and waited, gazing out at the three of them, wanting to see what they would do. The husband (and father) walked in. He sat down beside her and took her hand.

"What's this about?" he said. "Everyone's tired."

She ignored him. She turned to the children and shouted, "Hurry up! Get in here, the park's closing soon!"

They quickly climbed in, and the boy leaned against his father. The girl hesitated, unsure where she should sit. Su Qin reached for her, pressing the girl's ear against her heart.

The cup was slow at first, moving in time to a gentle melody. Then the music grew more impassioned and the cup spun faster. Su Qin felt as if she were being stirred faster and faster by an invisible spoon. The calm guardedness of the other three quickly melted away and each of their mouths seemed to have been shoved inside another mouth, from which came piercing shrieks. Shrieks that knew no tone or accent, but blended together into a yell that hung in the sky over the amusement park.

It was just as Su Qin had imagined. When the ride came to a stop, the four of them looked like an ordinary family, stuck close together, like four melted sugar cubes at the bottom of a cup.

Aminah

Note: By law, all ethnic Malays, including mixed-race Malays, must be Muslim. Applications to leave Islam are heard by the Syariah Court. Procedures vary according to state, but such applications are rarely successful.

IT WAS PROBABLY THE MEWLING of a cat that woke the warden. Then again, it might have been the wind. The wind blew through the doors and windows along the verandah, delivering anxious noises from the real world into the women's dreams. The warden had dreamed that a woman came up to her bed. The woman's face was in shadow, her features hazy.

"They've given you a place to stay for a while, that's all," she said. "But this isn't even a room. It's just the lights are off, and the darkness is giving you the wrong impression."

The warden tried to see the woman's face but could make out only a pitch-black strip of shadow, perched on the end of the bed. She stared for a while, unafraid, until a cold wind gusted in, making her shiver, and the woman disappeared into it. Then she heard the wails of the cats beneath the window and owls hooting in the mountains. Reality crowded back in, noisy and fragmented, pressing in from all directions. Long shadows skimmed the walls and pallid moonlight fell across the floor. It was a room like a box with a ceiling like a lid, sealed up. The door knocked in its frame and the warden sat up, intending to secure it. She glanced down the row of beds, where the women lay fast asleep, like a line of white cocoons. Only Aminah's bed was empty, the sheet pushed aside, pajamas crumpled on the floor. The warden started in alarm.

She could have stayed in bed, but instead she ran outside to look for Aminah. The verandah was cool and the lamps were dim. She groped around for her slippers and then hurried through the dark shadows of the building and the banana trees, heading toward the front gate. In the security hut, the guard was slumped in a canvas chair with his eyes closed. The warden rapped her knuckles against the counter and he woke up, peering blearily through the glass.

"Aminah's run off, I don't know where to," said the warden. "What if she's gotten out, or something's happened to her?"

"She won't have gotten very far, not at this time of night," said the guard. He adjusted his haji cap, clearly reluctant to move.

The warden understood. She really did. If Aminah was in her usual state, any devout Muslim would be ashamed to lay eyes on her. Ever since her stay at the rehabilitation center had been extended, Aminah had been acting out. The teachers kept trying to persuade her that it wasn't worth it. "It's all been decided, there's nothing you can do about it now. You have to face reality, Aminah."

Aminah, they said, had gone mad. She had torn off her dress, exposing herself. She refused to cover her head or study the Quran—not that she'd ever read it in the first place. One evening, she climbed into a well. According to the aunty who did the cooking, this was when the demon got in and sent her well and truly crazy. After sunset, the wilderness spirits get restless, especially in areas so close to forests. They creep out with the fog, in search of vulnerable prey.

The warden did not set much store by folk superstitions. Anytime a ghost story was playing on television, she'd watch until the most suspenseful part, then get up and start pacing around, making a show of her indifference; the Quran was more powerful than any sorcerer. But now, in the pre-dawn gloom, with the ghostly murmur of the wind brushing through the trees, the darkest, most nonsensical of those ideas rose from the undergrowth, along with the mist and the damp. A chill rolled out in waves, making her hair stand on end. There was a heavy scent of mangoes, pungent as the breath of an evil spirit. She pulled her shawl across the icy tip of her nose.

The grass had grown tall during the rainy season. Everything was black. She couldn't see clearly but knew where to find the well: beneath the mango tree, covered in weeds. No one used it anymore. It was centuries old; ancient forest dwellers had probably relied on it for water. It had existed long before the rehabilitation center. The land had been used as a military training ground for a while, then transferred to the religious authorities. They had built a garden with a boundary fence that ran along the edge of the forest, capturing the well inside.

Barbed wire coiled along the top of the chain-link

fence. As the warden walked, she kept an eye out for holes. It's not possible, she thought. There's no way she could jump this. There weren't any gaps and all the gates were locked. Aminah had to be in there somewhere.

Cats chased one another around the garden. They came into season, mated, gave birth to too many kittens. The cats could leave, but not the people. The people had to wait. Perhaps for three months, perhaps for one hundred and eighty days. Their arrival and departure dates were written in their files, the same way birth and death dates are noted down in Allah's *Book of Decrees*. And no matter who they were, none of them would stay as long as the warden. This was her home now; she could navigate the garden with her eyes closed. The wind roared behind the mountain and the sound crashed in like a breaking wave, but even that couldn't mask the shrieking of the cats. The kitchen was dark. The kitchen workers were still asleep. There was no sign of Aminah. She seemed to have vanished into the air.

The mosque started broadcasting the dawn azan, its solemn tones carving through the wind, and the warden went back inside to pray. One by one, the women rose from their beds and knelt on their prayer mats, facing Mecca, foreheads on the floor.

Do not fall by the wayside, the warden recited to herself. There is no god but Allah.

Another endless day, full of never-ending responsibilities. The trials would never be over, for there was no end, not until the end of this worldly life. She looked up at the window. The moon illuminated a cobweb over the glass. She heard the door creak, then open.

Aminah had returned. Her figure, in the gloom, walked the length of the dormitory, in front of the lined-up prayer mats. Every pair of eyes saw the soles of her feet, and the trail of mud and grass in their wake.

She passed by the praying warden, who lost track of her prayers. Aminah's fingers appeared frail in the moonlight, as if about to melt away. There was not a thread of clothing on her skeletal frame.

The women had stopped praying and were holding their breath, waiting for this naked, sleepwalking body to pass. They did not turn to watch her but listened as she moved around behind them. She climbed into bed. A thin sound arose from it; a gentle murmur, like the fizz of a carbonated drink, quickly absorbed into the long cry of the mosque.

The warden was shaken. Her internal recitations cut off. The women went back to their beds, but she stayed on her mat, trying to collect those fallen sentences, unsure where to direct her forehead. Aminah's damp tracks glistened on the floorboards. They were not quite fully formed footprints. Moonlight came in at a slant as the moon dropped behind the mountains. The majesty of the azan drowned out the echo of the wind in the valley and the cats' grating wails. It reverberated around the dome of the sky. She could no longer hear the crickets. No longer hear Aminah, or any other sound.

The administration had temporarily canceled afternoon classes, otherwise there would have been a line of students sitting in the dining hall, ready to repent. A coffee pot sat on the table. Coffee had splashed onto the tablecloth. To perceive a stain is to embed it in your heart; you can never wash it out. The rims of the cups were scalding hot. When they couldn't say what they wanted, they loudly sipped their coffee. They talked a little about everything but ultimately said nothing at all.

In the beginning, they had known only a few basic facts about Aminah. Born in 1975 in Baling New Village, Kedah. Paternal grandfather, Abdullah Ang; paternal grandmother, Xu Xiao Ying. Father, Hamza Abdullah; mother, Gao Mei Mei. Occupation and whereabouts of parents unknown. Neither appeared for the court proceedings. Cohabited with a non-Muslim male in Cheras district, Kuala Lumpur, at No. 35, Road 7/4A, Indah Gardens. Employed as, variously, a waitress, bar girl, and hairdresser's assistant. In 1993, applied at the Syariah Court to leave Islam. On August 20, 1997, the Syariah Court denied her request and ruled her still a member of the Islamic faith.

They had read her file aloud, giving voice to these details, but the voice had skittered across their brains; the moment the folder was shut, they forgot most of what they'd heard. And after that forgetting, they knew hardly anything about her at all. They remembered that she was from a Muslim family, had conducted herself in an immoral manner, had attempted apostasy.

Now, several months later, they knew a few other things. These were not written in the file. Aminah was wild and unruly. Aminah hated Islam. When Aminah sleepwalked, she could pick a lock with a piece of wire. What nobody knew was when this farce would be over.

"What else can we do?" asked one teacher. "How do we get through to her?"

"I give up," said the warden. "Even hiding the key doesn't work. Can't we send her away? She should be in an asylum."

Along the edge of the table, a wave of shaking heads. A few letters were passed around. A stack of documents shifted back and forth between coffee cups. All as quietly as possible. Someone repeated the warning that had come down the telephone line: "We can't send her away. Think about what they'll say. They'll say we did this to her. That we drove her mad."

"She's not mad, she just sleepwalks," insisted another teacher. "Sleepwalking is not the problem here."

"Well, then what is the problem? And what are we going to do about it?" The speaker's lips pursed over the rim of a coffee cup, pained and deadly serious. "Because whatever we're doing at the moment, it's clearly not enough." The table rocked slightly, as a finger knocked down to emphasize the last three words. "We need to ask ourselves some serious questions."

And so, for the next two hours, they went around repeating to one another those same phrases they had used a hundred times before: "There is no hiding from God." "We will bring Aminah back to the path of righteousness." "We will do our utmost to care for Aminah." "We will love and care for them all." "In this way, they will come to know Allah."

"This is His test for us," said one.

They all agreed, and started to eat cookies. Sparrows

hopped around pecking at their crumbs. The garden scenery was as familiar as always, seemingly impervious to the passage of time. Sunlight poured down and the shrubs quietly sprouted.

There were no walls around the dining hall and the light flooded in from all sides, blinding the teacher Hamid, forcing him to squeeze his eyes shut, as though he had been pulled underwater in the sea.

"We can't know everything," he said. "We're not God."

"It's true," someone agreed. "We're not."

So far, Aminah had only ever been naked while sleepwalking. When she was awake, she was fully dressed, sometimes weeping quietly to herself, other times talking softly. But when she sleepwalked, she stripped off her clothes and wandered around the garden. She was surrounded by fencing and barbed wire all the way to the sky. They were not worried that she would escape, they were worried that they might see her.

Beyond the fence was forest and wilderness. There was one lonely road, which had split off from the North–South Expressway on the west coast and ran deep into the peninsula's interior. Along it, transmission towers loomed over the vegetation, like used-up yarn shuttles dragging their last threads across the horizon. Evening mists settled quickly and dark clouds blew in on the wind. In the final waves of daylight, the horizon was as chimerical as fog, as far-off islands.

This was how it had looked from the car, when Aminah first arrived. She had stared and stared, until the power lines disappeared, and the trees, and the distant mountain range, all swallowed by the thick black fog.

When she entered the building, her limbs went soft and she could barely stand. Her insides felt like stones, piled to the top of her neck, and her legs were sacks of rocks that dragged along the floor. During the day, she choked on the unfamiliar food. At night, she lay in bed but could not sleep. They presented her with a white prayer dress and she hurled it onto the floor, then spat on it and told them all to go to hell. She yelled insults at anyone who happened to pass by. A little later, she allowed the dress to be placed at the end of her bed. After they gave up trying to convince her to put it on, she lay around sulking, muttering to herself in a language no one else could understand. She treated them as if they were invisible.

"Zombies," she said. "Pigs."

When she thought of the lovers who had abandoned her, of the relationships she could never make official, of that miscarried child, a crack spread through her body. It rose from between her knees and sliced her in two. It buzzed. Deep inside her forehead something shattered, and the noise sealed off her ears.

She buried her head in her pillow, feeling the cotton stuffing press back against her nose. My name is Hong Bee Lan, she told it, her voice sinking into the folds. They would say: *That claim is no longer valid, you cannot be Hong Bee Lan.* It had been read aloud in court, clear as day. No right of appeal. It was settled. No more changes.

Aminah.

Eventually, her hair grew long enough to hide behind. Her hair felt like all she had.

When Aminah had first arrived, she had still been willing to talk. Every so often, she responded angrily to questions, or pleaded tearfully with the warden, or erupted into broken Malay, trying desperately to explain herself. In other ways, she was just like everyone else, traipsing edgily in and out of the classroom. She too sought relief from the red-hot glare of the sun and the monotony of the dormitory, and followed the others as they shifted location through the day. Like them, she hated studying and never set foot in the library. No one did. They had been judged guilty of licentiousness, deviant ideology, gender confusion, apostasy, and forced into studenthood; none of them felt compelled to enter the library and thumb through tomes expounding on righteousness.

"If Muslim blood flows through a person's veins, they will be Muslim until the day they die."

The warden said so. Hamid said so. Inside the chain-link fence, every teacher said so.

"Aminah binti Hamza! All I'm asking is that you put your trust in God, is it really so difficult?"

Hamid was bewildered. The warden had asked her the same question, in the same tone. Inside the chain-link fence, the same question passed from one mouth to another.

It was a boiling afternoon, the breeze as indolent as a cow. The air beneath the fan pasted itself to the skin.

Hamid was drenched in sweat, a torrent of words spilling out of him as he labored to make his point.

"The Quran is perfection! Not a single word too much, nor a single word too little, because it was written not by mortal beings, but by All-Powerful God."

Aminah was distracted. She was so hot that her whole body itched. She was not wearing a headscarf. Her tangled hair hung down over her shoulders, and her exposed neck was covered in scratch marks. A few Orang Asli, who had also tried and failed to shed their religion, sat in the chairs beside her, heads lolling as they dozed off.

"Where is your scarf?" asked Hamid, keeping his tone cordial.

Aminah did not answer. She collapsed across the table, inert as mud, her matted hair like weeds.

Hamid recalled his colleagues talking about Aminah's volcanic explosions. He weighed his words carefully before speaking.

"If your boyfriend truly loved you, he would not have abandoned you. He isn't coming back, you know."

Aminah said nothing.

"And if your mother truly loved you, she would not have forsaken you. I don't understand—if they don't love you, why are you so desperate to go back? We love you more than they ever did. Why won't you let us in?"

Under the eaves, sparrows darted and chirped. Out in the garden, all the living creatures were stirring. Palm tree shadows flickered back and forth, back and forth, creating a shifting patchwork of light and dark.

At first, Hamid thought the wind was ruffling Aminah's hair. Then he realized she was trembling. She was hiding behind her hair, huffing and hissing to herself. Whatever she had concealed there, it was only a matter of time before it exploded. Her Malay came out in staccato bursts, but the meaning was perfectly clear.

"Why not talk to my father? That fucking pig, never gave me a sen. You! Are! All! Malay! Pigs! You're Satan! You get a toothache, you love Allah, I don't care—it's your business, not mine. Why do you care so much about other people's hemlines?"

Hamid could hardly believe his ears. Satan. He shifted from foot to foot, trying to think how to convince her.

"You can't say things like this. Don't hate God because you're angry at your father. Allah has plans for your father, just as he has plans for you. Promiscuity is wrong. Going around with nonbelievers is wrong. It will not make you happy, it will simply degrade you. If you cannot try to please Allah, your life will be utterly without meaning."

Aminah lifted her chin and stared at him through the black hair shielding her face. Her mouth drooped. She put her hands over her ears.

He avoided her eyes, letting his gaze travel down to her collarbones, where he could make out those faint, mysterious scratches.

"We will find our true reward in the afterlife, where there will be splendor even greater than that which we see before us…"

She would not accept it. This saddened him. He thought, This girl is unworthy of the name Aminah. "Aminah," a loyal heart. The bearer of this name should love and serve our God.

But still he felt compelled to save this lost Aminah, to rescue her from the abyss.

Aminah gave up hope. No one came. The outside world felt far away and she no longer raged or cried. After the first one hundred and fifty days had passed, the others brought in with her went silent too, leaving only the twittering of birds, high in the sky, and the rustle of wind through the trees. Ants climbed blades of grass, gnawing the edges as they went.

The court order for an extension of her sentence came. Another one hundred and eighty days. *It wouldn't have happened if you had behaved.*

The white cloth was bright against the warden's hands. It had been washed. It looked pristine. Obediently, Aminah pulled it over her head, covering herself right down to her feet. It was too big. The part covering her face shook with her breath. It felt like another layer of skin. This is where she would live from now on: she would wake up inside it, she would die inside it. Until Day 180. But after Day 180 there would be another one hundred and eighty days.

A black cave concealed each woman's face, and each woman dragged a long shadow behind her. Aminah dragged a long shadow too. Beneath her chin, on her chest, at night, it was as if there were someone lying between her and the women on either side. A gray person, lying between the beds, with a voice that leaped from their vacant body onto her mattress.

Aminah. Aminah.

Born again.

Was it all an illusion? An illusion, severed from the months, the years, the past. *You need a fresh start. The hammer's come down now, and it won't come down again. Why not accept that you're Aminah? What good is your old identity to you now? What good ever came of your past anyway?*

Their white gowns rustled against their bodies. They spread out their mats, knelt down, and in a few moments their foreheads were touching the floor.

After evening prayers, Hamid felt revitalized. He sat on the verandah sipping coffee, scooping out sugar from the bottom of his cup with a teaspoon. The clouds were low, almost touching the roof. He stared dreamily at the jade-green vine that curled around the verandah railing, entranced by the glossy sheen of its leaves. The long line of daffodils behind had contracted leaf mold and the flowers were slowly withering, despite the gardener's best efforts. Hamid felt sorry for them, but also felt that the world was progressing as it should. Allah's decree extends to every tiny detail. Allah the All-Merciful manifests His mercy in all things under Heaven. All living things have their place.

Hamid turned on the verandah light and started reading through the students' homework.

He did not remember the background of every student. He knew that one young man had returned from Indonesia and would expound at the slightest opportunity: "Read the book of Siti Hajar! Save yourself from eternal damnation!" A few others were instructors from religious institutions, sent to the center to correct their completely misguided interpretations of the Quran. Hamid did not understand how people could be so stupid.

An ignorant heart is incapable of discerning truth, he thought. That was the tragedy of it.

The more he read, the more he sighed. Not a single story was new; history just kept on repeating itself. One diary read: *The universe is Allah's dream. Dream? Siti received enlightenment from a dream. In this world of illusion nothing is real other than "me," for the illusion is born from "me," and therefore this "me" is Allah.*

It was absurd. It was astonishing that anyone was convinced by these obvious fabrications.

It continued: *Since everything is an illusion, what evidence is there that Paradise is real?*

They didn't believe in anything. Not in God, nor in honoring their obligations. Not even Paradise.

Hamid wrote, *One can see that a person without faith is noticeably more frail than a person of faith, for they have to live their lives thinking that Paradise is an illusion.*

Then, feeling that wasn't quite right, he crossed it out and corrected it: *Paradise is the place to which the souls of all true believers will return.*

The moon rose in the sky, then darkened.

A shadow fell across the page. Hamid looked up and saw Aminah. He was so shocked he almost knocked over his coffee.

Aminah's eyes were wide open but unfocused. It was immediately clear that she was asleep. She was sleepwalking but had drawn to a halt, as though sensing an obstacle ahead. She was not wearing any clothes and stood there before Hamid, moving neither forward nor backward, utterly exposed.

Oh Allah! Internally, he called on God for assistance.

He held his breath as he looked at her, bewildered by her body. All over her skin, on her breasts, her chest, her abdomen, were finely etched scars, like the veins in a leaf.

The evening rose up and closed around them, perching on the verandah railings. For a long, long time, the dusk was the whole sky, calm and windless.

Hamid's heart raced. The scars made him pity Aminah. He wanted to reach out and touch them.

Satan.

The enemy name flitted through his mind, sharp as a warning whistle. Just in time, he moved his gaze to the Quran on the table. Don't you know what she's dreaming about? Some confused thought seemed about to become clear, but then vanished back into nothing, like a wisp of smoke. Oh Allah, he implored again. His chest felt tight. He reached for the Quran but it weighed too heavily in his hands, and fell to his feet with a bang.

Hamid hurried along the path to the women's dormitory, damp, black branches scratching at the sky overhead, his unease like a scalding-hot coin against his forehead. I would never call a nonbeliever "Satan." Satan is Satan. A nonbeliever is a nonbeliever, they are not the same thing. But they get confused, he thought. The internal debate carried on: I have not failed, it's just Aminah's crazy talk, it's unsettling me. As Allah speaks through us, so Satan is always lying in wait.

This comforted him; he had preserved his Muslim dignity. Wicked thoughts are the same as wicked deeds, but then again, what counted as a thought? What if it was here one second, gone the next, left no trace? I have not thought anything, seeing as I was not in earnest. It was a moment of weakness, that's all. We must all be vigilant about nudity. One should not be naked aside from washing, visiting the toilet, or lying with one's wife. A man should not feel arousal for any naked body other than his wife's. Oh Allah, have mercy. If my mind must waver, let me be judged by my actions. I have controlled myself, prevailed over desire, and for that let us rejoice.

The heart is a battleground.

An evening wind blew through, sending dew raining from the leaves. Drops slid into his collar, cold against his neck. He felt calmer now. He saw the warden and collected himself, and briefly explained the situation. The two of them hurried back to the teachers' dormitory but Aminah had gone, leaving only a trail of muddy footprints along the verandah.

"You see," said the warden, "the girl is ruined. It's her nature, there's no changing it."

Hamid stooped to pick up an exercise book that had blown away on the wind, into a dip at the bottom of the steps.

"There is only one nature that Allah has instilled into mankind," he said. "And that is to rely on Allah."

The warden made no other comment and left soon after, muttering to herself. The air was clammy and the wind crashed around, rattling the exercise books on the table. Alone again, Hamid sat in a rattan chair, staring blankly at the page he'd been writing on before, covered in his black crossings-out and annotations. His mind was in turmoil. He wasn't sure what to think. Perhaps Aminah hadn't really appeared at all; perhaps he'd just nodded off and dreamed that she had.

The foil-stamped lettering of the Quran glimmered faintly in the dull light.

In his youth, during trysts with his girlfriend, Hamid had made sure the Quran was carefully stowed away in a drawer. He recalled one long-ago evening, just before he went abroad for religious training, his last chance to indulge. They had said goodbye, the shadow of the curtains swaying across their naked bodies as they embraced, teeth sinking into one another's skin, the marks deep but fleeting. And now that labyrinth of emotion soared all the way along those ten interminable years and landed on the table, flipping the strewn books. The lamp rocked in the breeze.

He opened the Quran, suppressing those old hurts and reminiscences, and started to pray.

The pitch-black sky seemed to possess a purity worthy of protection. And, much like looking for someone across the vast passage of time, the realization filled him with anguish. Yes, that was what he had to defend. That. In this worldly life, a pure heart is the most precious possession of all. Verily, Allah loves those who are pious.

How do things decompose, buried underground? The mud was acidic and stung the skin of unaccustomed city folk. When they rinsed it off, they found little red spots, which itched briefly and then disappeared. They were young and so they healed quickly; if they had been older…well, with older bodies death is always lingering overhead, gearing up for its performance.

Heavy rains came and flowers wilted, although new buds continued to sprout defiantly from the branches.

The earth was soaked. In the distance, a thick mist wound around the mountains. The wet season. Spores floated in on the wind and rapidly reproduced, covering logs and tree trunks in layer upon layer of fungus. A dead bird lay stiffly in the undergrowth, legs to the sky. Frogs ran away and cicadas screeched. Dead leaves industriously grew white spots, their rot bestowing blackness upon the soil.

New shoots surfaced through the mud.

In the vegetable garden on the mountain side of the compound, the women pulled up weeds that covered the ground like a net. Monitor lizards skulked along the periphery fence, provoking screams of horror. Even so, there were happy moments. If they cast aside thoughts of the restrictions and regulations, if they managed not to take them to heart, then these so-called licentious women, women whose moral conduct had been found so wanting, were perfectly capable of entertaining themselves. When the guards relaxed their watch, the women's shouts and raucous laughter echoed through the valley, mixing with the cries of birds and the wave-like hiss of the leaves, carrying to the other side of the dormitory blocks and dissipating into the wind.

The women loosened the soil and earthworms frantically burrowed deeper in, away from their shovels. Hamid preached.

"If all you do is read the Quran, you'll never understand. We have to experience it for ourselves. Only those of us who have planted seeds with our very own hands can comprehend: mankind is weak, but Allah is Almighty. It has been this way since antiquity. Mankind will gain nothing from going against the Will of Allah."

The sun came up over the men's dormitory, causing the single-story building to cast a long shadow across the men's side of the garden. The men were weeding, spreading manure, adding a layer of soil, sheets of newspaper, another layer of manure, another of soil. Layer upon layer upon layer.

The Indonesian student seemed to have forgotten Siti Hajar. He had been resisting all instruction, but now appeared engrossed in his weeding. Hamid took this as a sign that his recitations had done some good.

On the mountain-facing side, the women planted bits of everything—melons, beans, vegetables. Behind the dormitory, the men planted bananas, chili peppers, and taro. Hamid knelt down to pat earth around the base of a sapling, thinking of his grandmother's funeral.

"Planting seeds is called 'tanam,' the same word as for burying people," he told the students. "Planted seeds will sprout and blossom. After a person has died, their soul remains. To know where you will end up after death, you need only to reflect on your one, brief life, and ask yourself if your deeds and conduct have been pleasing to Allah."

All living things die and are reborn, he thought to himself, his frustration mounting. In a matter of weeks, we will harvest this garden. Is that when they will receive new life? Will they be saved? He continued to lecture, just as conscientiously as always, until the end of the session. The men exchanged glances among themselves, making furtive jokes or pulling faces, their hands caked in mud. No one was listening to Hamid. He wanted to yell but restrained himself.

Instead, he looked around at all those lost men, ones who had yet to be saved, and he pitied them. No matter that they had clearly indicated their disdain for his efforts to rescue them, still he would treat them with kindness.

"Aminah!"

One of the men suddenly shouted the name.

Hamid froze. Noticing that the man's eyes were fixed on a point behind him, he turned, but all he saw were low-slung sunbeams, the shadows playing in front of the dormitory, the deserted verandah. Nothing out of the ordinary. The swaying outlines of the trees, sparrows riding the wind, fat leaves flapping beneath them. But, as he surveyed the area, he realized that he wanted her to be there. He was scanning this complex world for Aminah, poor, pitiful Aminah, with her poor, scarred body. Somewhere in that familiar scenery, deep in the undergrowth, hibernated a creature both familiar and extraordinary. It was in the shadows, sleeping endlessly beneath the wide-open sky. For a moment, the silence was complete and all-encompassing.

He felt that Allah's grace and mercy were truly present, descended upon all things and all living creatures, and that holiness and corruption were but a hair's breadth apart. He wished there was no guilt. The thought seemed to arrive out of nowhere, a longing that rose like water in his chest, so that he almost overflowed.

He wanted to speak but there was no one to talk to. Nowhere to go and say the things he wanted to say. Instead, he silently turned to face the lost men, squatting in the dirt of the vegetable plot. And there they were, of all ages, from all backgrounds, each one scouring their surroundings for the legendary naked Aminah.

The tales grew more fantastical with each retelling. In the kitchen, the cleaning lady and a huddle of students whispered about the sleepwalker's supernatural ability to free herself from constraints. It was a gripping thought, at once tense and exciting, although they dropped it after a few sentences, fearful of summoning evil spirits. But this underlying dread seemed only to propel those sentences further and faster, sparking an ever greater desire to listen and fabricate. At the staff and teachers' meeting, they considered the potential damage of this belief. They could not completely disregard it, because in Malay folk tradition the roots of this kind of superstition ran deep. Neither could they hope to eradicate it, when it was so embedded in people's minds; superstition was something they clung to for reassurance. And so they held a meeting to discuss it, and the meeting ran off and on for an entire week without nearing any conclusion. They searched the Quran for guidance, for a clarifying verse, but opinions differed widely. The debate continued until their shared faith and unity seemed to teeter on the brink of collapse. To avoid misunderstandings, they agreed to pause proceedings until the principal returned from holiday. Hamid, that promising young teacher, the one they had always looked to for solutions, felt his interest waning, and slipped wordlessly away.

Aminah was always back by morning. One day, she returned seeming exhausted, as though she'd been walking for miles, and quickly fell asleep. Weeks passed without any further escapades and the warden dared hope that the farce might be over, just like that.

For several nights in a row, the warden woke in the early hours of the morning. Unable to fall asleep again, she would listen to the soft fizzing of rain on the roof. It pattered onto leaves and soaked the window panes. Everything felt muted. One such night, still bleary, she noticed a cluster of dark shadows hovering around Aminah's bed. Instantly alert, she tiptoed over and found three sisters from one of the northern provinces, performing an exorcism. They sat cross-legged around the bed, spat into their palms, and began chanting under their breath, the chant interspersed with violent exhalations. After a while they brought their palms to their mouths again, exhaled sharply, and then returned to their recitations.

The warden reprimanded them, keeping her voice low and restrained. She tried her hardest to seem reasonable, even kindly, but the women paid no attention. And so the warden felt her temper rise, forcing its way from her chest and emerging as a sharp, hard voice.

Even that voice was not enough to stop them. They had been transported to another world entirely: their eyes were open but they did not see. They kept repeating the same actions, over and over again, as though possessed themselves—a circle in the air, a wave, hands back to mouth, spit, chant, exhale, arms out again, a circle in the air.

The warden gasped in horror. The thought flashed into her mind: They are all possessed. She looked around the dormitory and saw that several beds were empty. Not only those belonging to the three sisters, but others too. There were bedsheets tangled on the floor. She stepped back, despairing and terrified, and quietly fled the room.

Oh Allah, protect us.

She fled into the rainy night, where all she could see was a tearful sky and tearful trees. The treeline penetrated the deepest part of the darkness, where cricket-chirps and owl-hoots blended into one another, like garbled fragments emerging from a cave. She hurried along the damp path, clutching an umbrella, feeling the icy moisture on her toes. Water ran off the umbrella onto her back and shoulders. She passed through the circles of light beneath the lamps, speeding up in the shadows, heading toward the security hut at the entrance.

She rapped the counter with her knuckles.

The guard was sitting idly behind the glass, just as always.

"Gone," she said. "Run away."

"What?" replied the guard.

"I don't know! I don't know what to do," she said, stumbling over the words. "They're all possessed…"

The guard did not react as she had expected. He didn't even yawn, simply stared at her blankly. She stepped back, her whole body shaking. The guard's eyes were heavy. His expression was unsettling, although she couldn't say why. The small circular speaker-holes drilled into the glass blurred his mouth and nose.

She returned to the path. A cat shrieked in the courtyard. Every so often, she heard the thud of fruit against a dry roof. A quick bump and then gone. Dead leaves fell as silently as passing time. It was an exceptionally black night, the moon as slim as a fingernail clipping. She sat on the wooden staircase outside the dormitory, her back to the line of narrow doors along the verandah. She knew the sounds coming from behind them, knew they were from the women who had stayed inside, who were still lying in their beds, sleep-talking and grinding their teeth. That's how it was all night long; enough to give you goosebumps if you woke up to hear it. She did not want to hear it anymore. In front of the steps, wind whipped up the fallen leaves, blowing them crisply across the concrete.

She closed her eyes.

Time passed, and she opened them again.

Her eyelids were so dry that she could almost hear them blink. Her hand still gripped the umbrella, and the umbrella was bone-dry. There was no rain on the concrete. A chill swept from the top of her head all the way to her toes. She wanted to stand but her legs and bottom were too numb to move, as though she'd been leaning against the railing for hours, not just a minute or so. Her shoulders ached and her neck was stiff. She touched her headscarf—one of those soft, shiny ones. She had never worn one before.

Aminah, she thought. Sleepwalking Aminah. It was as though something came and sucked all the clothes off Aminah's body, peeling them off and dumping them on the dormitory floor.

The wind blew in from who knows where. The sky was full of stars about to fall. She shivered with cold but resolved to withstand it, tried not to think about it—in fact, she couldn't have done anything even if she'd wanted; she had to wait for the numbness to pass.

The crescent moon tilted, gradually sinking behind the mountains. She watched, conscious that this very moment was the darkest, the one just before the sun rose.

Aside from the few lamps in the courtyard and the patches of light in the guard's hut and the prayer hall, everything was black. In a moment, the dawn azan would start. It would drown out the voices of those ten thousand unknown beasts and insects in the mountains, its holiness resounding up the river and inland to the deep recesses of the jungle.

She attempted to recite lines from the Quran in her head, but the only thought that came to mind was this: Pious souls flow like water over moistened ground. Nothing else. The moonlight was very weak. She looked at the black ground. It looked so deep it seemed bottomless.

Wind through the Pineapple Leaves, through the Frangipani

Note: The name "Aminah" is very common in Malay society; as with Sarah or Mary, there can be many Aminahs.

A LIGHT BULB SWAYS beneath the eaves.

An idea floats up, making my heart pound. I want Aminah to run away. But her mind is somewhere else, hanging upside down, the sand in her brain flowing into the top of her skull. A frog-like person appears; let's call them Bi. But Aminah will only notice Bi once they have swum up the hourglass and surfaced from the sand. And now Shaimah's coming over and Aminah's sipping bitter coffee. Let's try again: an amphibious person appears. An early morning dream. Aminah does not remember the rest. She opens the door and sees a pair of webbed feet.

Shaimah wants to be Aminah's friend. She brings over her diary for Aminah to look at. I encourage Shaimah to thrust the book into Aminah's hands, but Aminah has not yet come to her senses. She flicks through the pages, the words shuffling to the outer corners of her eyes and then onward into the dull light of the torrentially rainy afternoon.

Imah misses her ibu, her ayah, her little brothers. Ibu, when will you come for Imah? A lot of new people have arrived. Ibu, don't be angry. Don't be shocked. Imah has something to discuss. Imah wants to get married now. She can't study anymore anyway, school's over for her.

A dead frog lies at the foot of the table. By the time Aminah sees it, it's squashed flat. Smaller than a petal, maybe only recently born, one little foreleg pasted to the black floor. It looks like it snatched ahold of something in its final moments. Its dead webbed foot is flat and dark and disproportionately huge.

Aminah looks at Shaimah. Shaimah is two years younger than her.

"You really want to get married?" she asks.

"No," says Shaimah, embarrassed. "Imah is just saying. Aidah went home. The day before yesterday, her parents came up to the fence and started shouting, saying she had applied to get married. They brought the certificate to show Kak Roni and so Aidah got to go home. Imah wants that too."

Aminah looks at "Imah." She has one hand resting on her belly and the other supporting her waist. She arrived four months ago, looking just a little plump. Her parents brought her in and never came back. In the months since, her body has expanded like cooked rice. Yesterday, the warden took her for a check-up. The nurse said the test was negative and the warden screamed like a madwoman in the clinic. "It's not possible! It's got to be wrong, it's got to be."

It's time Shaimah got married, but who will her husband be? Not the policeman who raped her; she hates that son of a bitch. Sometimes she cries hysterically in the evenings. Sometimes she gets so desperate that she pulls out her hair. But she calms down whenever there's singing.

Aminah's thoughts turn back to herself. She's been here four months. The new court ruling came the day before Hari Raya Haji, decreeing that she should stay another four. Aminah did the math: one hundred and twenty days, two thousand six hundred and sixty-six hours. Rain gurgled through the drains. She ran into the parking lot.

"Come back here!" shouted the warden.

"I'm waiting for someone," said Aminah.

"No one's coming, it's not Saturday."

Every two weeks, Aminah meets her mother in the parking lot. Her mother hasn't been able to get her out yet. Marrying her off would be a good strategy—after all, who better than a nice Malay husband to honor her Malay mother, and who better than a nice Malay husband to make sure she keeps faith in Allah. But if Aminah were willing to do that, there wouldn't have been any problems in the first place. Aminah does not want to get married. She would rather die.

Bi surfaces from the quicksand just in time to snatch the words from Shaimah's exercise book through Aminah's eyes. Aminah sees that everyone else has written Shaimah sweet little messages. *Dearest Imah, may you be happy always. Happy Birthday*, over and over again, big and small. Pages and pages of it. The authors seem to have used the square guides in the middle of their rulers to write in, because all the letters are perfectly even. This confuses Aminah, but then she thinks, Well, if no one writes to

Imah, Imah must write to herself.

Then she reaches a page where the neat blue writing morphs into a messy scrawl, scratched right across the staples in the middle of the page.

I hate myself, I hate that I was so stupid, why did I listen to that policeman? Why? Maybe I was afraid of what he would do to my family. Almighty Allah, deliver me from this suffering.

Aminah feels a vice squeeze around her chest. Her eyes are misty again. The sky never seems to brighten. No matter how many times they wash the windows, it's always gray behind the window's lattice. A webbed foot sticks to the wall and silently glides past. A webbed hand is like fog: it can't show Aminah the way. Fog seeps through the windows and onto the floor. Aminah watches it swallow her knees and the table legs, watches it swallow the dead frog.

The coffee on the table has gone cold. The women's afternoon coffee break is almost over. These days, none of us like to look at the clock. Our fingers make more sense than our eyes. When the coffee is cold, it's the men's turn to come in.

The men sit on the left side, the women on the right. The men have their entrance and we have ours. Neither Aminah nor I ever let our eyes glance in their direction. Seventeen-year-old Junaidah is always dawdling in the middle, her headscarf ending in sharp points over her breasts.

The wind flings open an exercise book lying on the ground.

It was flimsy enough to start with, then Shaimah went and ripped half the pages out. The ones left behind are falling out now too. Her handwriting is very ugly and jumps all over the place. That's right: Shaimah does not like studying, and neither do Aminah and I. School wasn't much better than here but at least Kai was there, and we used to sit up talking all night long, before the sun came up, when the lights were out. We talked like that for two years without saying anything at all. There were things I wanted to know and things I could not say and things I absolutely did not want to hear.

In those days, I wanted to flush Aminah down the toilet.

Ants are carrying crumbs down the table legs. Can they tell that they're not horizontal anymore? A straight path extends from the crown of their heads. Once again, Aminah feels the sand flowing into the crown of hers. Her neck bends. A webbed hand industriously scoops the sand away, as though preparing to plant a vegetable.

The rain keeps everyone a prisoner indoors. Outdoor activities are on hold, no one is allowed out, there's nothing to do other than read aloud from the scriptures. Or copy the scriptures onto a stack of flash cards and then glue them to the wall, until the wall disappears. Or polish the floor and windows, over and over again. Or watch religious films, like *Virtuous Maria* and *Memorial Day of the Battle for Southern Thailand*. In the evenings, the girls lie on their beds, scribbling in their diaries.

At first, Aminah refused to write a single word. She would press her head into her pillow. She did not believe any of the friendly messages the others were writing. Who wanted to remember this hellish place anyway? No one takes their diaries with them when they get out. They chuck them in the trash outside, into the jumble of empty jars, plastic bottles, and plastic bags. The rain makes the ink run.

And yet still the warden does her rounds, gathering them up. Who knows why. They sit in a pile on top of the cupboard behind the library sofa.

Who knows if anyone ever reads them. Who knows if the ustaz really pray for us all. Maybe only Allah knows, Allah the Almighty. We can stare all we like, but only He knows whose eyes are truly reading.

Supposedly we won't be here in the valley much longer. They are looking for land to build a bigger, better House of Faith. Then we'll leave and so will they. Sooner or later, every single one of us will toss this valley to the back of our minds. We'll leave this never-ending rainy season right where it is and stride off down that sloping mud- and horseshit-splattered road out of here, without ever looking back.

The wind spins on the road.

"This horse is blind," I say to Aminah. "The light's too bright, it can't see anything."

Our hands entwine in front of a candle. A shadow horse canters over the floorboards, through the vacant glow of the flame. A few seconds and it's gone. It had a hole for an eye. In the candlelight, our hands are very white and the shadows are very black, engulfing the corners of the room.

"It's run somewhere deep, deep inside," says Aminah. Her eyes follow it into the darkness. The horse only had a head and a neck, so we can't watch it run.

"You hear that?" I ask.

"Hear what?"

"Hooves."

We saw the horses when we were driven in, although at first they were almost invisible through the evening rain. One horse galloped around the pasture with its head down and its neck twisted, and gray clouds piled onto the ground around it, as though taking it prisoner.

"If it was nighttime, you'd see them asleep standing up," said the driver. "There's no need to tether them, they just stand by the fence. They're good horses."

The car wound its way up the little mountain road. When it reached the fence, one of the guards got out to open the gate. The gate was heavy and its rusty corners scraped noisily across the pavement. Perhaps that would have been the moment to throw open the car door and escape, but we just stayed sitting there like a corpse. Anyway, there was another guard in the car with us and she gripped Aminah and me tightly by the shoulder, her wrist like iron.

The car passed through the fence. The tires had to churn through piles of horseshit to reach the iron gates of the House of Faith. Every morning, those good horses carry their masters past the gates and up the mountain. We hear their hooves disappearing into the distance along the rocky jungle path. Clip-clop, clip-clop, like a band of cheerful drummers, loud and crisp and then gone.

"They're asleep. They won't be running around at this time of night."

"You're wrong," I say. "Don't believe everything that

driver said. There's a horse out there, listen—clip-clop, clip-clop, clip-clop."

"Well, then it's a bad one," says Aminah. "Or else a blind one, that can't tell the difference between day and night."

The wind spins in my brain.

sementara = temporary

How long is "temporary"? How long before it doesn't count as temporary anymore? Time flips like a coin. Wake up, sleep, wake up again.

"It's so meaningless," I say.

"No, it's not," says the teacher.

"God's love is the rule," says an ustaz.

"We must delight in God's love," says another. "If freedom amounts to nothing other than satisfying one's base cravings, one's nafsu—well, then renounce this freedom."

The wind blows across my father's father's grave, trembling on the Qingming pineapple leaves.

nama = name

There is a creased line where the ceiling meets the walls. It's like the room has been torn apart and stuck together again. It's like being inside a totally different room.

There's a game that goes like this: say a person's name out loud. Swap names with them. Don't stay attached to your old one. If someone calls your new name and you don't answer, or else calls your old one and you do, then you're dead. There are no second chances, dead is dead. Instant elimination.

"You will take the name Aminah," I heard the ustaz say. "It means 'a loyal heart.'"

Barbed wire coiled along the top of the walls. The hammer came down, banging April into a long, long chasm. A voice shouted from it: "Aminah, Aminah."

Born again.

A hand passes through my brain. A 5 a.m. wake-up. The call to prayer booms across the sky, the sound like an enormous bell crashing behind me. I follow it onto Aminah's prayer mat.

The wind carries the shouts a hundred thousand miles, all the way to the Gombak River.

I drag Aminah here and there, and it's like dragging a heavy iron hammer. I want to smash everything into tiny pieces but cannot muster the strength. Eyes slide over me as I stand in the garden, cursing like a mad old woman. "What are you looking at! Don't you all have cunts of your own?"

My elbows used to be hard as rock. My neck bent for no one. Maybe people talk behind my back, but then again maybe they don't. Maybe they say, "Poor Aminah, she's even more wretched than that girl Maria." Let them. Maybe all that pity makes them feel better.

The curtains are heavy. Water drips from towels hung over the indoor washing line. The doorjambs are moldy.

The name Maria is like a spear stabbed into the ground at my feet. Back in the 1970s, Maria was a white girl with two families fighting over her. Her adoptive parents were Muslim but her birth parents were Catholic. The case was heard in the Netherlands and Singapore. The straw mat we sit on, in front of the television, is divided in two, one side for men, one side for women. The light from the screen flickers on our faces. We watch the case of virtuous Maria. All the shouting is dubbed. The subjects weep as they tell of how they have been wronged, robbed of love and honor. The voice of the narrator roils in the background, as though there's a raging furnace in there. It's not just in the past; the fires are stoked, even now.

The name Maria is like a spear tossed past me, sharp enough to slice off a toe. Maybe it has. I feel like I'm missing something, as if my foot is no longer my own. Behind my back, the others are probably spitting out pronouncements like seed husks: "Aminah's more broken than Maria." "Only the greatness of Allah can make her whole again."

Maybe we only know half of Maria's story, just as we only have half of mine.

The wind makes the doors knock in their frames.

"*hari depan* = afterward," writes Aminah. I watch her write.

The clock is wound. Tick-tock, tick-tock. The sand flows thickly. Another day. Another week. It's yesterday and it's tomorrow.

Aminah can only write a few simple words. They are not my usual words, but everybody says they will be with us all our life. And who knows how long an everlasting life might be. Should an everlasting life be spent draped in a prayer robe or with hair draped wild and free over one's shoulders? Should an everlasting life be lived with endless freedom to strive or is that freedom, when all is said and done, just another illusion? Does an everlasting life mean a life spent racing across constantly shifting ground?

During the everlasting rainy season, we all sit together and stare dull-eyed at the square glow of the screen: endless grassy plains, the dog-eat-dog world of the African wilderness, a snake swallowing whole a chicken thrust into its cage. A deer running like the wind, a flock of geese migrating from the southern hemisphere to the north, their cries gradually fading into the distance. Aminah's eyes are wide. A vast world where there is no need for language, a world untouched by humans. If only. She writes: *That is the other shore.*

Later, in the classroom, she half-closes her eyes as she copies from the board.

The board is green and the twisty Jawi script is written out in white chalk. The sentences are short but the time is long; it hardly seems to pass at all, like it's backed up forever and ever inside this room. Today's lesson is on minor sins. Yesterday's lesson was on major sins. Inside Aminah's exercise book, sins are ripped apart and torn out, held like a bunch of uprooted mimosas, dropped in the trash when her hands start to ache. Time is like a wheelbarrow ploughing through soft mud, rolling down a hill.

Reading from the Quran mends mouths, but they sin by mispronouncing syllables. They sin by secretly skipping pages. They sin by lying. They sin by gently pinching someone else's palm, and sin by pressing someone else's face into their laps and trapping their hair between their knees, stroking their head. The scent of wrongdoing wavers on their lips. The corners of their mouths collapse inward, forming two sharp little caverns.

It is all major. As major as the crumbs carried by the ants.

The wind blows the rain sideways, blows clothes sideways. The clothes never dry.

muram = desolate

It's the day before Hari Raya Haji and everyone has gone home. Only Aminah is left behind. Every hour the warden comes looking for her with eyes like pincers. The emptiness weighs on Aminah. It feels like she has swallowed a bowl of stones, or maybe a spiky fruit. Her lungs, heart, stomach are empty rooms.

On the day of the festival, starting from the dawn azan, she spreads herself as wide as the garden. Or, to be more specific: for the whole day, she walks and scatters herself. Her skull splits into four parts. One part sleeps on her pillow, one falls into a washbasin, one is forgotten in front of the television, and one is left behind on the sewing table.

Her tongue stays behind in her cup. Her toes lie on the doorstep. Her elbows rest on the edge of the dining table. Her mouth slides inside her pencil case. Her eyes press against the window glass. Her fingers are wedged behind the bolt for the gate. Her knees roll off the top of the fence. Her ribs fall into a clump of flowers. She can't go any further. The outside world is a hundred paces beyond her fingers. Aminah is everywhere.

When she wakes up, she'll realize that this is all a dream. The difference between dream and fantasy is that the latter might cheat you, but the former never does.

The evening of Hari Raya Haji, Bi arrives at the edge of the compound. That night, noise crashes through the jungle. Some of the sounds have names: owl, window, bucket, leaves, wind. But others do not. Panic and listen all you like, but you'll never know for sure whether they're of this world or not.

Like the horse. It sounds like a horse: clip-clop, clip-clop, clip-clop. It paces through your mind, as though it's come inside the fence.

I first saw Bi in a dream. There was skin between Bi's fingers, very soft. Cutting it out was painful and there was no point anyway, because it kept growing back, layered with scars. A hand webbed like a fan patted lightly against a harmonica. There wasn't much of a tune, but all the way through what passed for one, I heard the knock of those hard-hard scabs, keeping the beat: tip-top, tip-top, tip-top.

The wind pulls hair straight and puffs jacket pockets.

bahagia = happiness

My dearest abang, how are you? Are you eating enough? Drinking enough water? Are you well? Do you miss me?

Here the writing is spiky and tall, different to how it was before. This book has a lot of pages. Does Shaimah have a boyfriend to call "abang"? No, Shaimah does not. This isn't her handwriting. All through the interminable rainy season, the girls write down their deepest longings, although their only readers are each other. As their books are being read, the authors turn to look bashfully at the wall, as though the wall has the power to calm them. Rain patters against the other side. If they don't know what to write, they write song lyrics. *If you've never loved, you've never existed. Heaven, if you can hear me, turn these feelings into rain.*

To: Zhang Mei Lan.

In July, my mother brings me a letter. It's from Kai, and it begins: *Dear Mei Lan, how are you?*

The rain stops for two weeks. The world becomes almost transparent; the mountains seem to retreat. I've landed in a circle of glorious light. I want to open my mouth wide and scream into the wind and feel my voice sucked into the high and distant sky. I imagine galloping like a horse. But it's not time for me to gallop yet. The boys are playing football in the field. For now, the field belongs to them. For now, the girls belong to the vegetable patch.

Just one little jump and I could be hanging upside down in a tree. Sway, sway, a newly planted daffodil blooming in my brain. *Ah, ah.* Blue sprouts from the branches. My feet kick about, kick about like crazy.

It's not just because of the name.

In August the valley is sodden once more. Out in the parking lot, Aminah looks up into the rain. It falls in silent needles from the sky, then shatters noisily against the ground. A pregnant cat drags her heavy belly across the lot, the poor thing. This weather is so boring.

So boring that visitors don't show up. Aminah feels like all the sand inside her head has collected on one side. It takes a long time to return to normal and in the meantime she leans against her pillow, writing laboriously, one stroke and then another, sobbing poor thing poor thing poor thing poor thing until she can't write anymore. Two candles cast her as two shadows. Why are we so strange? She bites my nails, staring fixedly at the wall. A spider climbs across her blank gaze, as if climbing up a tombstone. On the third day after Hari Raya Haji, at five in the morning, the wind blows the doors open and Bi comes in.

We notice Bi at the same time, in front of the prayer mat. When we lift our forehead from the floor, we see a trail of damp, muddy footprints leading to Bi's long, webbed feet. Bi is a gift from above. Heaven's answer to our prayers. Bi is all sinew and bone, dry and shriveled, scales almost too big for her body, like a frog just returned from the desert. Why does Bi look so strange? With our back to the light, we watch Bi fade away, like watching a shadow fall across a mirror. Who made Bi like this, amphibious, dual, neither of earth nor of water? This is the question, hidden like frogspawn in the sand of the hourglass. We did, is the answer. Aminah and I. And the understanding undoes us, what to do, what to do. Go back to yesterday, the day before yesterday, the day before that—time is like a steamroller, crushing everything flat as a card and vanishing it into endless blackness. Aminah and I prefer to pretend that Bi fell from the sky. Fell like rain from on high. Imagine how far Bi must have come.

The wind blows umbrellas away. They turn somersaults across the grass, rolling to the edge of the compound.

lari = escape

It's hard to say whether this story is being written by me or Aminah. Sometimes I help her edit the story line and sometimes she tries to correct my wording. But most of the time we can't tell which of us thought up which sentence. It's the same when we try to work out where Bi came from. It's impossible to know anything about Bi's ancestors. At the very beginning, one of them must have fallen into a river (surely it would have been a river because the ocean is far too big) and then slowly moved toward dry land. This ancestor followed the coastline, kept on going through swamp after swamp. Swamps are good at swallowing footprints and also at swallowing names.

This is a bit sentimental. Maybe everything we think about Bi is wrong. After all, we've never really thought about people who exist between two elements before. Take us: I never even wanted to think about the existence of Aminah. I have a crazy fantasy that Bi is our guardian angel. I have it even though the ustaz say this is a Western idea, that angels are servants of Allah, and our webbed friend is too lowly to compare. But I can't control my fantasies. And so the amphibian sleeps by our side, with rugged scales and hardened scabs. The dream closes in on us, damp and cold.

Loneliness is to blame, there's no doubt. Bi appears to me as someone small and thin, but in my fantasies Bi is tall and strong. Without even meaning to, I rely on my fantasies to lick my wounds. It can be a clear and sunny day or the depths of the rainy season and my loneliness doesn't go away, so the fantasies just keep on coming. Maybe it should have toughened me up. But it's like a non-stop carousel. Loneliness, exhaustion, fantasy, disillusionment. Fantasy fails and you're confronted with reality, and the reality is that you're lonely, and you have to get used to it. But you'll never overcome it, because it's tiring to be lonely and exhaustion sets in, and then the whole thing starts again. Should this be making me stronger, this perseverance in the face of the same ordeal, over and over? If I believed in God, I wouldn't need to battle this alone. But if I choose not to believe in God, then loneliness is my own burden to bear. Does that make me pathetic, like a poor dog begging for scraps? I think it's more pathetic when a person does not dare to ask questions. You don't know what you should ask, so you prefer to stand as far away as possible. You prefer to believe whatever it is you have to say to make yourself feel better.

To be honest, I don't really want to tell Aminah's story. She always makes me feel pathetic. But there are some things that have to be done, whether we like it or not. In this story, Aminah is more obedient than I could ever be. I'm good at running away, although not at fighting back. When I want to run away, my gaze shifts outward, alighting somewhere else, for example on the fluorescent light in front of me that's switched off now, a thick gray line like the crease in the wall.

When I ask myself questions and answer them, Aminah disappears and Bi vanishes into a little crack, or maybe dips back underwater. I dream up a little hideout for Bi: fireflies glow faintly on all sides, mossy rocks steep in ink-black river water, whirlpools gurgle and slap against Bi's ears, slap-slap, slap-slap, as Bi drifts further and further away. Bi drops like a lead weight into the wild dreams of some Chinese ancestor of mine, fleeing his enemies all those years ago.

The ancestor lands on solid ground and is terrified. He

pulls out a knife. At the edge of the field, he sees a huge, long-horned monster, ferociously charging toward him. He uses the knife. He races down the dirt track and villagers chase after him, brandishing their sickles and hoes, seeking vengeance. The field is vast and there's nowhere to hide. He runs as fast as he can, until eventually he reaches a palace. The sultan is out for a stroll in the flower garden. He takes one look at the ancestor's sorry state, and the hordes of angry villagers behind him, and says, "I will protect you, but afterward you will be my child."

A newborn frog hops in the road, no bigger than a raindrop. Roads criss and cross. Shoes tiptoe over puddles. The hemlines of long skirts rise and fall, rise and fall, white socks, black shoes.

The wind masks the tip-tap, tip-tap of footsteps.

Two people escaped. That's what all the girls in the dormitory are saying. Their voices come and go between the washbasins and their towels, brushing softly against the mirrors. The light bulb's been dead for a long time now; three whole months. Everyone gathers around a candle. The wardens aren't here. It's ten o'clock and the front gate's locked.

They looked all day. They searched everywhere.

It's not actually that hard to run away. Or to climb over the gate. The hard thing is choosing where you run to.

"McDonald's, KFC," says one girl. "Whatever happens, you won't starve."

I shrug Aminah's shoulders. Aminah, I call. I scratch at her chest.

Aminah looks down at her feet, as if I live in the tips of her toes. It's easy for them and hard for me, she thinks. They were voluntary admissions. If they don't find them, they'll drop it. If I disappear, all the police and TV stations in the whole country will know about it. Like the court case.

Aminah's hands flex in the candlelight. Her horse is almost blind, the light's too bright. Looking straight at the light, you can't see anything at all. Bi squeezes a webbed hand in between us. Bi's hand shadows don't have eyes, which means Bi's hand shadows aren't very good. Most hand shadows have eyes, at the very least a little hole to let a bit of light through. Look at the wall. There's a blurry shadow flying around, though it's hard to say what it is. Bi's shadows are always racing around in a panic with their eyes closed. Sometimes I understand perfectly well that Bi is not our guardian angel. Maybe Bi is something more like a totem. But totem isn't the right word either. Bi exists. Bi is very close to us, even if Bi does act like a ghost who can never step into the light. It's not only me and Aminah who dream of Bi. If Bi is not a collective blindness, then Bi is a grain of sand in all our eyes. Bi is a house we all abide in, a road we want to go down, our prayer mats, luggage, clothes. Bi's voice is low and raspy, traveling straight from my mind into Aminah's: You'll have to be clever about it. You won't be completely free but you might be a little bit.

Of course, you'll need a bit of luck too.

Bi gives very little. That's all there is.

The wind surveys the highest point in the city.

When Bi runs away it looks like Bi is jumping out of

her own belly. Bi's clothes are like nets. Bi escapes from a dream and flashes through the streets, very much alive, passes through forbidden doors and does forbidden things, very much alive. Bi has two faces, Bi is two things at once, and this saves Bi.

It's said that this place was originally an army barracks. Gunshots are always sounding along the periphery. Even in the rainy season, the drills go on. Shouts ring out from the jungle. I picture the mud on the soldiers' boots. The fingers pressed against their temples.

Could those long, webbed feet jump over the fence? Aminah doesn't know. Aminah sees a pair of long, webbed feet suspended in midair, a light jump and then they are flying, webbed toes spread wide.

In midair, in midair, and then down.

Owls sprout from the treetops. They fly off without making a sound.

A big gutter, an overgrown little path. The fence is just a layer of wire netting. Behind the wire netting is a little path. To the left are the mountain barracks, to the right is the main road down the mountain. There's a bus stop at the side of the road, where you can catch a yellow minibus straight to the northern train station in Kuala Lumpur, where every street is lined with fast food places advertising for workers.

I don't care what people say about me. They don't know what I'm thinking. And I don't care who they say I am, Aminah writes angrily in her book, *I am who I am.*

First you have to free yourself, says the tip of the nose. You can only be angry so long before your nose gets blocked, as if you've flung it into the sea and the salt water has come in to drown your heart and lungs and stomach. The exercise book is creased, hot and damp and wrinkled from the weight of our elbows. Bi's webbed hands pat at a harmonica and the harmonica huffs beneath Bi's gills. There is a chill, a trembling, the trembling flips the gills over. I want to love, says the tip of the nose, hotly, acidly. If hate means that I can't love, well, then I truly am in prison.

The wind blows through the balsam flowers.

"The baby's coming," says Shaimah. "He's kicking me."

No hand can make a shadow shaped like a person. It has never been done. You can't make a person. That patent belongs to God.

Stand up and you'll see it. The candle makes your shadow grow. When the wind flickers the flame, Aminah sees Bi hopping and dancing on the wall. The girls behind her are singing. They start out low and quiet. They only have one song. *Night falls and I'm all alone, let me wash away the sin and I'll come home. In the silent night, I wash alone, oh may my lusting heart be bright again.*

Every so often they forget the words and giggle to fill the gaps, then resume the song. *Why are you a hazy shadow, why am I a fish chasing bait?* The air is damp and stuffy; the doors and windows are open only a crack, because too much of a breeze would snuff the candle. We cup the flame in our hands. *The winds have passed now, don't tarry on the seashore. Don't entrust your hopes to dreams, because you'll wake up with nothing.* The candle casts flickering shadows onto the ceiling. The roof beams are like bones holding up the night. There's a girl crying with her head in her hands, saying, "Sorry, sorry." All through the long, long rainy season, the girls have been waiting for rebirth, rebirth. *After rebirth, I will not be who I was before*, writes one.

A vine climbs up to the roof, silently wrenching open a crack in the wall. The white daffodils bloom in July and are washed away by the September rain.

"Aminah, what do you think of Ustaz Hamid?" asks Shaimah, under her breath. "Every evening when he recites the scriptures, Imah wishes she could grow wings and fly to him."

Aminah listens, her mind blank. She stares at Shaimah's belly, then up to her face. Then back down to her feet.

"Aminah, don't make fun of Imah! He doesn't know," says Shaimah. "Imah wants to love and she's fallen in love with Ustaz Hamid, who knows why."

She's talking nonsense, I hear Aminah say to herself. They force us to love Allah and it confuses people. Aminah faces Shaimah. She manages not to say anything, but her puzzlement provokes me. I squeeze back inside her eyes and settle at the top of her nose, looking out at Shaimah. Shaimah seems to be holding back. She also seems to be smiling. Her lips are twitching at the corners, her nostrils are flaring, she's leaning against the headboard of her bed, hand pressing on her stomach, breathing deeply.

"It's shameful to be pregnant like this," she says. "Minah, maybe you hate the ustaz, but Hamid is different. Aminah, Minah, don't look down on Imah, Imah hates being laughed at. Sometimes Imah forgets her own big belly and the child inside it. But every time I forget, he kicks me."

Shaimah rubs her belly again.

Aminah closes her mouth. Crickets chirp. The song swells beneath the ceiling. *O Allah, free me from suffering, grant me peace.* Neither Aminah nor I pay much attention to Malay songs. They all blur into one another, the syllables as indistinct as the cricket noise. But suddenly I find myself listening, and the song I thought was about God turns into a love song—no, maybe it was a love song all along. *In the misty evening, I long for his shadow. In the dusky twilight, a tide rises in my chest.*

I drag Aminah around, I loathe Aminah. Once, I wanted to give birth to a different self, in order to dilute her. But every time it seems I could be rid of her forever, I hesitate. It is so hard to decide. What if one day I want Aminah back? Unless I could run far, far away, to continental Africa, the grasslands of South America, the feet of the Rocky Mountains, places like that. Places from a dream, where there are no regrets, from where I could never come back.

The wind blows across my mother's mother's grave, shuddering on the frangipani.

Every fourteen days, I meet my mother at the pavilion in the parking lot. She always arrives on time and she's never once missed a session. When I sign my name in the register, I count, and she's been nine times in total. My father, only once. I don't know if this is because he doesn't want to or because he's not allowed. We get very few visitors here. Sparrows fly low over the parking lot. The guard is crouched beneath a faraway mango tree, smoking. Gleaming white smoke drifts behind it, the trunk slick-black from the rain.

"I've been so stupid these past years, dreaming such stupid dreams," says my mother. "The time has come for me to wake up. I can't stand the way he looks at me, like I owe him something. I never forced him to do anything!"

"So when can I come back?" I ask.

Her face falls. It's old and wrinkled, as if thoroughly wrung out by the years.

"Once you get out, I'll help you change schools," she says, after a long pause. "You can go wherever you like."

I want to tell her that there's no point, but after turning it over in my mind, I say nothing. For someone like me, all the schools will have the same sharp spears. They want me to stay here nine months. It doesn't matter to them that this will set me back a whole year behind everyone else. I try to imagine the place I want to go, once I'm out. What I hoped for, a long, long time ago. No ustaz, no warden, no one claiming to have my best interests at heart. I want to go far, far away and be reborn, like a child. I want to give birth to myself.

"Any letters for me?" I ask.

"No," she replies.

She looks at me, her gaze landing on my face like a handkerchief. I probably look terrible. In the damp, cramped little pavilion, bathed in light so blindingly white that it seems to pierce through everything, we look at one another and eat the food she's brought, but don't say much else. People always say that we're mirror images of one another; that looking at one of us is like looking at the other through a mirror with a time lag of twenty years. I look into that mirror hoping for guidance, some sign of what's to come, but it's a mystery. I can't see through it, and neither can she.

The wind blows across shoes drying in the sun.

Luck can't stay bad forever. Two cats snarl nearby. They've been fighting long enough that both their ears are bleeding. A fruit thuds onto the roof and then rolls off onto the ground, where it will rot before it has the chance to ripen. A dead bird lies with its legs to the sky. Aminah looks everywhere for a good omen but there are only bad ones.

Whatever the omens, no more letters come from Kai. Everything feels unbearable. The world spins fast and it's flung me out of its orbit. This separation is pointless. His name peels away from inside me and I want to scream it. Water sours in my chest. I look at the trees, look at the blank road ahead. The wind loosens rainstorms from the leaves. Stand at the railings and you can feel the whole valley is dripping, the rain turning everything black: window lattices, tree trunks, roofs, pillars. Birds build nests in holes beneath the eaves. Spiders are massacred and then reborn, lurking in the corners of the ceiling while their legs grow long again. Cat shit stinks up the garden.

Shaimah's gone to have her baby. The warden's at the hospital and now there are just two lazy guards, crouched under the mango tree with their cigarettes. They'll stay there smoking for a couple of hours, then go and make their rounds.

Wring out a cleaning rag and hang it over the railing. Pick up the shoes that have been drying underneath.

They're still a little damp; tie the laces together and drape them over your shoulder.

The wind bangs open an exercise book.

Bi's webbed hands bring me a sleepwalking horse. A swaying black horse with its eyes closed. It gallops very quietly, as soundlessly as shadows moving on the ground. When I sit astride it, it carries me away like a time machine. The two guards don't even notice us as we pass right in front of them. At most, they notice a slight breeze, something moving in the garden, here one moment, gone the next. Everything is as it should be, and no one will remember that there was ever an Aminah here. In the files, there's a blank space where her name used to be. They might find that puzzling, might wonder what used to be there, in that emptiness above the line, or wonder where all the exercise books on top of the cupboard have gone. Later, maybe a passer-by will wonder where all the people went, and what kind of place was here before it turned to rubble. Here in this valley, on this abandoned plot, by then all covered in broken glass and trampled grass. They might feel a flash of curiosity, but it won't linger long. They won't figure it out, not unless they really go chasing after answers. And why would they? We're not high-profile cases like Maria. We're lost causes, forgotten dreams, that's all.

Press your bare feet into the stirrups, grip the reins, squeeze its stomach with your legs. You have to learn to handle a blind horse; don't let it buck you. Maybe I'm blind too. Freedom is a flower of kicked-up dust as you gallop down a mountain: stop moving and it's gone. I want to run far, far away, to a place I've never been and no one knows about, and live a life free from desire. It's not that I'm not afraid. Who knows whether

I'll succeed. Whether I'll manage to vanish from this place, so that they hear no news of me ever again and cease to know a single thing about me.

You have to be smart about it, I say to Aminah, still unsure who is leading whom.

Aminah is very quiet. She doesn't say anything. She's temporarily mute. Where to now? Where to go for a peaceful, untraceable life? To no longer fear being alone? So long as I fear being alone, I will never be untethered, there will always be neighbors, friends, lovers. Desire will sweep me away again and send me back into the net. Then there'll be no avoiding it, I'll have to turn into someone else, but who? Aminah? Zhang Mei Lan? Maybe neither. Maybe they are both impossible. Who knows what kind of thing I'll be by then. But if it doesn't matter who I am, why not banish myself right now, and carry on being Aminah?

No, there has to be a choice. If I love somebody, I can choose whether to be like them or not like them. Maybe one day I'll be Aminah again, maybe not. This is all so hard to predict. How am I supposed to know? I don't even know when I should leave the valley.

The best destination is probably the savannah. Yes, that's it, then we could really run away from it all. But then again, I'm not sure I could bear to be completely forgotten. It's hard to say, will this calm us down or break our heart?

At the thought of being completely forgotten, tears well up. The Gombak River flows a long, long way. Why so sorrowful, why so reluctant to leave?

Anyway, all we have is this blind horse. Pass through a forest that crashes like the sea, follow the Gombak River down the mountain. Stroke the horse's ears, press bare feet into the stirrups; I have to learn to handle a blind horse. I feel that Aminah and I are bound together like a thick scab plastered over a throbbing heart. Sunlight explodes from behind the trees and dazzles my eyes. Aminah, I call. She abides in me, still and quiet, and later we will be each other's secret, one that neither of us can deny. The horse is quiet, the stones are smooth, the forest is thick, the coast is far away.

For a second I watch a blade of grass. I do not move. I watch a wavering thread of light for a long, long time. When you don't say or think anything, it's like sinking into mud. Once everything is completely gone, I'll speak from my heart, right into the air. Please blow away my longing. Slide down this slope, follow the expressway, traverse fields and lichen-encrusted mounds, pass through container ports, climb up slopes, rise above thundering freight trucks and jangling train rails, blow over the grass by the tracks and scatter the sand from between the sleepers, one grain at a time, don't stir up dust, keep on until you get to his house. Knock over the fence and pass by the orange trees. If the stuffiness is getting to him, he'll appreciate the breeze.

After a while, the tree-sea roars. The wind swoops down from the tall, tall sky and lands on top of me.

The rain stops for two days and the leaves start to rustle as they walk. Aminah and I sit very still and quiet, drying our toes in the sun.

October

"This would lure him on for many a night to come to dreams of sea and wide horizons."

— Yukio Mishima, *Confessions of a Mask*

A NORTH WIND. A quiet as sturdy as a cliff face against the ocean.

The sea breeze blew across Kikuko's temples and inside her flower-patterned collar. October, season of shifting winds; of winds in chaos. A southwesterly in the morning could turn to a northeasterly by afternoon, making it a perilous time for voyages at sea. Set off for Sulawesi and you might end up drifting toward Palawan. Venture into the Pacific and you might never come back.

In the balloon, it would be calm to start with, because it would sit inside the wind. But then would come a pause, a switch in direction, a sudden breath of warm air. The earth would spin in giddy circles down below—roofs, ship masts, people; all bright as stars. The bay a blue plate, revolving slowly from west to east, and the air silent, undetectable except for the currents dragging you along, pushing away the shoreline beneath your feet. Ocean waves would knit together and surge forward as a blazing, shimmering expanse.

It was the wrong season for flying, but Sir Kimson Wings, highest-ranking official in the North Borneo Armed Constabulary, would not take no for an answer. Hans, the Dutchman, had informed him that conditions were most stable over Sandakan.

"The wind is changing," said Sir Kimson. "It'll chuck it down soon."

"Rain's no problem," said Hans. "There's, there's plenty of hot air."

"It won't fall? Good to hear. Kikuko, you first. We can put a trapeze in, you can swing around under the basket. You'll love it!"

Bullshit, thought Kikuko. Aloud, she said, "But my dear sir, I thought all I had to do was stand in the basket while we made a quick loop around Sandakan? And then didn't you say there'd be a magnificent ship, coming to take me for a sail?"

"Let's shake it up a bit! Set Sandakan on fire, give people something to look at. Maybe one day they'll set up a balloon championship," replied Sir Kimson.

A dozen assistants were scattered across the lawn around the balloon, each holding a bamboo pole hooked to a net over the lower half. They kept the casing taut, lest the air flow stopped and the whole thing collapsed in flames.

Despite the breeze, Sir Kimson's whiskers glistened with sweat and damp patches extended along his back and under his arms. A long white tube, perhaps for a telescope, was slung across his shoulders. He stepped into the basket and made an exuberant little turn; there was room for three or four passengers. Kikuko peered up into the balloon and saw a small burner with a glowing yellow flame.

"To go up, just, just turn up the fire, and up she goes," said Hans.

Hans was short and slight, with eyes that rolled upward as he spoke, as though to watch a film playing inside his head. He explained how to light the fire, direct the hot air, open and close the deflation vent.

"For steering, I apologize, but there's, there's not much you can do with this kind of equipment," he said. "Not unless it's a Zeppelin. And, unfortunately, I don't know about Zeppelins. Only hot-air balloons."

"Who cares?" exclaimed Sir Kimson. "That German dogshit can go to hell!"

"Yes, yes, too right. Germans, no point in that. Float, just float away, it's the purest feeling of all, leaving the earth behind."

Kikuko listened demurely, clasping her parasol. The burner hissed. What would it feel like to fly in this thing?

The balloon was very big and the burner looked far too small to inflate it. They waited a good long while, but the casing remained slack. They waited until a fine drizzle rustled against Kikuko's parasol. Darkness fell.

"Shit, you goddamn celaka!" fumed Sir Kimson.

"No need to stop," said Hans. "It's fine, the burner's still going."

But it was no use. The drizzle blew in sideways, cold and wet against their exposed arms and toes, and the balloon's red fabric slowly shriveled. Then a gust of wind came through and defeated it once and for all, toppling it across the dampened grass, where it lay splayed and enormous.

The burner went out, and they had to drag the whole contraption across to the shed, out of the rain.

Kimson stared at the blurred gray lawn, his eyes glazed with boredom.

"It had better fly tomorrow, palui. For two weeks you have been wasting my time and money…"

Hans wrung out his hat and put it back on. The resulting creases made him look slightly comical, as if he had a dishcloth on his head.

"Perhaps, the balloon, somewhere, a leak," he said. "They can be hard to find, because the layers—there's taffeta, paper, more taffeta…"

"Are you a man or not? Fix the fucking leak! Or don't you even have the guts for that?" bellowed Sir Kimson.

Sir Kimson had a face of thick black whiskers, which made him look a lot like Jesus, as depicted in paintings around town. He had lived in North Borneo for over thirty years, which was even longer than Kikuko. Earlier in his posting, he was stationed in Api, where his arsenal of guns made nearby pirates piss themselves in terror. Even the notorious Caos, the father-son duo that had been rampaging across the South Seas for more than three decades, had been terrified into submission; they had vanished shortly after Sir Kimson had arrived. He had only recently been transferred to Sandakan. His troops included Ceylonese and Bengali soldiers, as well as indigenous Dusun. The latter knew the terrain and were famed for their tenacity and endurance, making them expert at tracking escaped prisoners.

There were all sorts of rumors about Sir Kimson, each one painting him as a terrifying force of nature. Even Kikuko found herself racked with nerves in his presence.

But her pulse still quickened whenever she recalled his tenderness at their very first meeting. They had been at church, and he had knelt down to free the hem of her skirt from where it had caught on a pew. At every meeting thereafter, he became more and more of a mystery to her. Kikuko felt like she was interacting not with one man, but with a host of different people, all sprung from the same root. Inside Sir Kimson were children, elderly people, young men, even a few women.

Sitting beside him now, Kikuko was uneasy. The flames in the brazier felt like they were burning through her temples. She knew what it was, bubbling away on top. The house doors had slammed shut. The butler, who usually lurked gloomily around the drawing room, had slipped away somewhere. Over the last few weeks, the housemaids had been dwindling, and it made Kikuko suspicious: Was Sir Kimson eating them? She thought of the dinner party on her first visit to the house, when a petrified kitchen girl had dropped a plate of roast chicken and turned as green with fear as someone facing a firing squad.

Although, in truth, Sir Kimson was not overly fond of guns. He preferred whips and doing things "the good old-fashioned Malay way." Which meant that after the whips came salt, immersion in the river, nails, mud, and earthworms stuffed into the seven vital apertures of the head.

"The old aristos were real gila babi! Crazy, crazy pigs!"

he declared. "Sat around with their fat bellies, inventing rules. Pity they're all Muslim now. It's all just about inheritance these days."

He poked a scalding metal stick into the bowl of a very long pipe, then gently shook out a clump of black paste.

"Anyway, death is too good for that cocksucking governor and his monkey secretary. He doesn't know who I am. Exile him to the desert islands! Let the savages give him hell."

He said nothing further. He inhaled deeply on the opium pipe and let thick white smoke curl from his nose. His eyes turned soft and contented. A little while later he passed the pipe to Kikuko, raising his chin in her direction. At first, she was reluctant to take it. Then, without quite intending to, she complied. Smoke coiled gracefully before her eyes.

The letter that had made him so angry danced in the flames and was swallowed up.

Time pitter-pattered back and forth. A map hung on the wall. Kikuko knew that it was a map, but not what it showed. It might have shown Japan, because Sir Kimson had once said to her, "You see it? That little prick that's flown out of the trousers and come down splat in the Pacific? Your damned emperor is a little crotch louse, creeping in bush hair from the day he was born. No brain, no balls, and he thinks he can take Shandong!"

Now he threw her onto a strange chair, curved like an enormous cow horn. In an echo of its splayed lines, he wrenched her legs apart.

"Getek cunt!" he said. "Idiot telingung woman. Whore."

He always shamed her like this. Desire rose in her

forehead and rolled in waves to her groin. She feared him but she wanted him. She wanted to caress him and soothe away his troubles, but he didn't mention them again. It was as though he'd never even laid eyes on that enraging directive from the governor general's office, now ashes on the table.

The final smear of sun across the window made her think of the altar in St. Michael's church. The countless Sundays she had spent enduring those interminable sermons, delivered in unbearable, incomprehensible English. And here was this rogue with his garble of Sulawesi, Hakka, and mixed-up English words. The church English was too exalted for her to understand, but understanding Sir Kimson's only served to humiliate her.

The evening mist had settled in. The only light came from the little opium brazier. There he was, stark naked now, towering over her, God, they looked so alike— Kikuko was frightened again. Sometimes, fantasy took over and she could believe that Sir Kimson and Pastor Chiu were two little children cleaved apart by the events of August. She watched his skin ripple as he thrusted and imagined the soul inside it. Instantly, she was boiling hot and shuddering, on the verge of passing out.

If you despise me, she thought, I can't bear it, it hurts, it hurts…

It made her want to die. Her world was trapped between two dark currents. When Sir Kimson released her, they moved to the Persian rug, where he fucked her hard. This version of Kimson was uncharacteristically sweet, and Kikuko sucked at him as thirstily as a newly hatched insect.

Growing a chrysalis was easy; retreating to a cave and

sleeping until dark was easier still. But she felt old, and that if she kept on being fearful, the gates of time would slam shut forever. So she had done something she would never normally have done: she had scraped off her shell and risked throwing her whole body into the open. It felt like she had stripped off her clothes and hurled herself into a ravine, where the mud along the bottom was soft but full of thorns, growing as frenziedly as weeds. One brush and they sank into her bones, making her body froth and bubble.

Since September, she had made up her mind: even if it was not just her imagination, even if those thorns were real, she would love them.

The rain grew heavier, into a crashing shroud. She felt a sudden, consuming urge to go somewhere far away. But she knew the sky would be no different, and so she stayed inside the pouring night. Dry land was a long way off, but paradise was near.

She could see the rain pooling in the grooves of the windowsill. The rolling roof tiles beyond looked close enough to touch.

"Slut," said Sir Kimson. "You're wet enough to sink a boat."

When he hurt her, she fell to the bottom of the ravine. But then he would be considerate again, and she'd gently float back up.

It isn't real, she told herself. Sir Kimson is Sir Kimson, Pastor Chiu is Pastor Chiu. Once the rush of the opium wore off, her earlier anguish swept back in. She studied Sir Kimson's face as she put on her clothes.

It was the cheekbones, she decided. The cheekbones

stretched out the lines of his cheeks. Add to that an intense, concentrated gaze, a pair of protruding lips, and that was both their faces, almost mystically identical. Oh, they are so alike, she thought. Maybe I'm the only one who's noticed.

She'd known Sir Kimson for less than two months, since August. He had walked ahead of her down the church aisle and sat at the opposite end of her pew. By that time, Pastor Chiu was already on the ship home. To win support from friends, he'd said. He planned to stay three months and take the next season's ship back. But he'd be off again before long, leaving Sandakan for Canton, to join Sun Yat-sen's alliance.

Kikuko had intended to have a quiet morning. And she had, until she saw Sir Kimson's face; then she felt caught on a hook. When she walked out of the church that Sunday, she was so unsteady that she almost fell down the stairs.

Pastor White, devout man of God, could not have imagined that by urging Kikuko to pray, he would be thrusting her into the arms of this knighted monster.

Early the previous year, Pastor White had paid his first visit to what people called her "coffee house," to talk to her about Jesus. He came quite a few times after that, bringing psalms translated into Japanese, which he would read aloud: "O my soul, thou hast said unto the Lord, Thou art my Lord: my goodness extendeth not to thee." For the most part, Kikuko was unmoved, although there was one sentence that made her so indignant she had to laugh.

"Thou hast redeemed my life."

It was not that she wouldn't like to believe it.

"But I've already redeemed myself," she said to Pastor

White. "How can God redeem me again?"

She had come south over twenty years before and had a decent grasp of the native tongues, as well as Hakka and English, but the never-ending weekly sermons were difficult to follow. At the very end of February, just after Chinese New Year, Pastor White appeared once again on Japan Street. He told her that he had found a pastor fluent in Japanese.

This new pastor was from Taiwan. He'd spent the previous two years in Api and only recently moved to Sandakan. He had gone straight to the Basel Mission, and they had agreed to lend him the church kitchen for his services.

The kitchen was quiet on Sunday mornings. There were very few believers: seven or eight workers from the Japanese-run cacao plantations, among them two Chinese from Taiwan. Kikuko attended with Kusa Noriko and Hanaga Yoshiko; the three of them walked over together, or hailed a rickshaw, turning off the main port road onto Singapore Street, geta sandals clacking as they approached.

They sat upright and very still, at the far end of the long kitchen table surrounded by chairs. Light flooded through the back door. A faint chill carried in on the morning air.

In early March, Kikuko had arrived and observed the pastor stand up and smooth down his clothes. She remembered it vividly. He had gone to retrieve some booklets from a cloth bag hanging from a pillar. It was early morning, but already sweat was staining the fabric under his arms. For some reason, she found herself staring brazenly at those big damp sweat patches, until he felt the weight of her gaze and spun around.

She felt a rush of shyness.

He observed her with childlike intensity. He introduced himself as coming from Keelung.

"Another port," he said. "The mountain road is just as steep as here."

He wrote his name on a small blackboard with a piece of chalk: Chiu Shou-ching. He had a neat, clean-shaven face. He was very learned. There seemed almost nothing he did not know, from astronomical geography to indigenous folklore, and Kikuko grew used to listening to him from the far end of the kitchen table. There was a purity to his character that she had never encountered in anyone else. Much later, she was finally able to find words that described the strange feeling he inspired in her: it was like opening a window in a pitch-black room.

She thought of the Amakusa Islands. She had almost forgotten her hometown, but still remembered its hard, dry sand. The earth in Amakusa was hungry and it swallowed a lot of people. People died chewing sand. There were more dead people in the ground than there were live rats above it. Her house had been as dark as a rat hole and, in it, her mother had grown weaker and smaller by the year, as if gradually sinking into the earth; as if there were something on the soles of her feet, pulling her in. One winter she decided that she no longer wanted Kikuko around. Kikuko drank a little ginger tea and left with a stranger, onto a boat going somewhere else. "If you don't like it, jump overboard," said her elder brother. Ten-year-old Kikuko did not jump overboard. Though death was scarier than hunger, her stuffy wooden box was scarier than death, but she wasn't allowed out of it onto the deck.

Thinking about it now made her feel abandoned all over again.

But she had not been abandoned, she told herself; she had abandoned them.

At first she had thought it was wrong to feel sadness about her departure, but she was starting to think it might not be. She felt melancholy, a mood that hovered like a cloud of fog.

She didn't know many Japanese characters. A few katakana. Kanji that she studied while the pastor was giving his sermons, one stroke at a time. How miraculous that he knew Japanese, even though he wasn't a real Japanese person. Was it a sign? Was this what was meant by "God's call"? Although God's call was contradictory, because all those holy stories and verses wanted people to give thanks, but also for them to quake with fear. God was somehow both loving and furious. Take the Denial of Peter: "Before the cock has crowed, you will have denied me three times." How Peter must have suffered that night.

It was troubling sometimes, but still she preferred to sit in the church and feel troubled while surrounded by its holy embrace. One glimpse of Pastor Chiu's welcoming presence was enough to suffuse her with hope, at least for a little while. Then would come another cruel part, and the fear returned. Fear and happiness swirled together like a cyclone. But do not deny, do not resist. Heaven has its ways.

In May, Kikuko heard about the Xinhai Revolution for the first time, and Pastor Chiu started to talk about Dr. Sun

Yat-sen. She was familiar with the name; in those days, even the rickshaw coolies had it constantly hanging from their lips. In the office attached to the church, a few of the Hakka board members had hung up a photo of him, and it was not uncommon to see people bowing respectfully before it.

It was a troubled year in Sandakan. Sometimes, Kikuko would leave the house in a cheongsam, and switch her geta for cloth shoes with pointed, bead-encrusted toes. It was not a very good disguise. The Chinese girls had single eyelids and sallow skin, just like her, and a similar aura of being old before their time, but most of them wore unlined jackets and cotton trousers. They would emerge from the plantations filthy and disheveled, with their faces peeling and their bones jutting out. Some didn't even have shoes, and went around barefoot.

The previous May, Kikuko had been heading away from the port, down a pepper vendors' alley filled with a jostling, shoving crowd, when a rainstorm swooped in and soaked them all to the skin. She dropped her umbrella. The Dusun and Indian guards appointed by the North Borneo Company pushed into the crowd and began arresting Chinamen distributing flyers around the docks. A southwesterly wind swept the alley, pushing past feet, quickening footsteps until people seemed to be riding the air. Kikuko ran with everyone else, racing for the far end. The rain was heavy and the ground was slick, and the rickety bamboo shelves leaning against the alley walls, used to dry peppercorns on sunny days, came crashing down. The crowd hollered and screamed and pressed on through the chaos. A cart became untethered and rammed into Kikuko, pushing her through a doorway.

It was another kitchen. Dark and clammy, cave-like. Inside, a frail old man was asleep on a hard wooden board, his face like a skull. She tried to ignore him. He was probably just another coolie with an opium habit, attempting to ease his suffering.

At first, she felt nothing; not even the slightest flicker of pity. But then she noticed that he was looking at her. There was a faint glimmer in his eyes. Her heart clenched. She had never done a good deed in all her life.

There was no one there to see, which made it easier, although it still felt stupid to do it—she made the sign of the cross and whispered the psalm, "Thou shalt be a crown of glory in the hand of the Lord, and a royal diadem in the hand of thy God."

He blinked, head pressed into his hands. He didn't flinch. She reached for him, intending to touch his forehead, but stopped halfway. Through the mottled brown window glass, she could see rain beating on the road, hurtling feet churning the surface to mud, panic everywhere.

She left when the rain stopped.

That afternoon, she started planning to do something honorable. She decided that there should be a church for Japanese people.

Pastor Chiu was not Japanese, Kikuko knew this. Pastor Chiu was a Chinaman. He was always talking in the Minnan dialect to the Taiwanese believers. Kikuko couldn't understand much Minnan and so found it strangely comforting, a compensation of sorts, to observe his interactions with the Chinese Hakkas from the Basel Mission.

He sometimes gathered with them to sing hymns; other times, to argue fiercely. He was always a little aloof, a little lonely. Sometimes he would suddenly get up and leave, or start leafing through his book, or break off from the group and walk by himself. As it was, the Hakkas never walked in front of him, in their twos and threes—they followed behind, leaving a space in between. Among themselves, they were a chatty, boisterous group, whereas the pastor was quiet. He didn't seem to depend on anyone. He was on his own.

This jealousy and secret delight was not rational. Kikuko knew it was not good to think like this. The pastor was the pastor. He was not Japanese. They might live in the same town, but they did not share a hometown. He was a man of God. But, sometimes, she dearly wished they had a shared heritage to bond over.

Kikuko didn't know if anyone else was like this. She watched Noriko and Yoshiko, wondering whether they felt the same things she did. She considered her own life, her piles of rashly accumulated jewelry and cosmetics. Meaningless, all of it. Flashy stuff that would just tarnish or be forgotten. She marveled at her former ability to spend money like water; at her blithe disregard for her finances and her body, the unpaid debts stretching back over a dozen years.

Her transformation made her delirious with happiness. Pastor Chiu helped her to accept some of the more uncomfortable Bible passages. The ones about original sin, and the terror of Judgment Day.

Since coming to the kitchen prayer sessions, Kikuko

had reflected on her former suffering, and concluded that it was a blessing to have encountered the pastor. This was God, allowing her to come closer to His grace. Every time she prayed, she gave thanks with all her heart. She would silently mouth quotes from Proverbs, her peace of mind for the day depending on the ritual: "A merry heart doeth like a good medicine, but a broken spirit drieth the bones." She was also fond of Nehemiah 8:10: "Neither be ye sorry; for the joy of the Lord is your strength." She couldn't read many characters but could recite these lines by heart, and doing so lifted her mood. It made her feel gentle.

At first, all was well. For a whole year, things were peaceful and she felt none of the fretfulness that used to push her toward frivolous purchases and ostentation. She was nothing but respectful toward the pastor. Starting from the new year, despite the continuing dire state of her finances, she instituted a new policy on Japan Street: the brothel would close on Sundays, and the girls were free either to take the day off or to go and work elsewhere.

Partly through fundraising, partly through direct donations, by the May that Pastor Chiu started talking about Dr. Sun Yat-sen (a year after the incident in the pepper vendors' alley), Kikuko had raised enough money to build a chapel in the western part of Sandakan. It had an attap roof but a Japanese-style wooden door, and was raised from the ground on squat mud and stone blocks. The front part, a space of about two hundred square feet, was to be used for services. A large stove was built in the kitchen, containing three separate ovens, and there was an outhouse for the latrine.

The chapel was surrounded by hundreds of acres of Japanese-owned coconut and rubber estates, and a little farther away, over toward the mountains, was the Manila hemp factory, also run by a Japanese firm. It was a long trip from St. Michael's church and Japan Street, but much more convenient for the plantation workers.

One morning, Kikuko came in with Noriko and another girl from Amakusa, to make a start on the cleaning. She ran a cloth along the base of the walls, working it back and forth until the floorboards gleamed. The windows were open, a mountain breeze gusted in, sparrows and cicadas chirped.

She drew water from the well and scrubbed and soaked and scrubbed again, washing the cotton sheet she planned to use for the altar. Eventually she wrung it out and hung it over the washing line. The sky was a limpid blue. She couldn't tell whether the wind was blowing in from over the sea or somewhere inland, but either way it felt refreshing. She retreated under the shadow of the eaves, and the wind grew stronger. The distant clouds were like ships, sailing up from behind the mountain and pressing forward, flinging her aside into this still, dark shadow.

After a while, she went back inside. The kitchen was silent. The girls had gone to walk up a nearby hill, where there was a view of the hemp factory and its young Japanese laborers. She went into the front room and lay down on the tatami, feeling thoroughly exhausted. Just a few minutes, she thought. An aging yellow flame tree stood outside the open window, its trunk covered in moss and its petals trembling in the dappled sunlight.

She stretched out across the tatami and relaxed. She was so tired, she was only intending to do as she usually did: to say a few prayers of thanksgiving, then rest for a moment.

And whatsoever he doeth shall prosper.

It was a peaceful afternoon. The trees cast swaying shadows and weeds quietly grew. She closed her eyes—oh! Her own body startled her.

Oh Lord, if only it wasn't a sin.

Pastor Chiu's voice seemed to ricochet off the walls. For a moment, she could clearly visualize him: his face and body floated before her like watery shadows, and he bent to meet her eyes. It was just past midday, and light flooded through the windows of the newly built chapel. Perhaps it was just that her arms and legs were stretched out. It was so comfortable. She rarely allowed herself to relax. Now she was lying flat on her back, limbs loose, and—oh, there it was. A breeze climbed over her ankles and skated up her calves. It was round like a ball, there and gone, there and gone, until it reached the top of her thighs and paused, circling.

She lay very still. It was delightful, gently nibbling like a fish, sending soft, soft waves through her legs. At first it was only a gentle throbbing, and she allowed her legs to fall open, ever so slightly, and everything was slow and drawn out. A restless warmth crept from her stomach down to her thighs. It was as if an invisible pair of hands were working to and fro. But the hands weren't just invisible; they weren't touching her. She felt an intense need to respond, but then felt she should resist. Except the stiller she was, the greater the trembling in her body, like a rising sea, until she couldn't bear it any longer and she flipped over, a body spinning inside a wave, and she pressed the wave between her legs, feeling the seaweed firm against her.

It subsided.

She opened her eyes. Sat up. There was a large damp imprint on the tatami. Such base thoughts. She was shocked; had not expected something as chaste and desireless as giving thanks to turn into something like this.

The sun was tilting west. Her mind felt as if hung from the iron spokes of a rickshaw sunshade. A thread sprouted from her forehead and started to pull, tangling around the wheels that ground over Singapore Street. The long road twisted around dramatic bends, mountains on one side, sea on the other. At some point, she became aware of Noriko, roaring like a tiger in her ear.

Kikuko stared in confusion.

"Am I invisible?" complained Noriko. "I'm going to the pasar for a bit. Do you want some kueh?"

Kikuko went back to running the brothel as usual. There were accounts to be done. Things to take care of. When people called her, their voices seemed to filter through from a great distance, further away than Heaven. She wished they would leave her alone.

At the beginning of June, Pastor Chiu set sail for Taiwan. The brand-new chapel had been used only twice, and now it was being left to the birds.

On Sundays, she still went over to sweep and pull up weeds, staying until the afternoon. Occasionally, Pastor White came to find her in the coffee house, inviting her to come back and pray in St. Michael's. She dragged herself to a couple of services. At least there was no one to bother her there. As soon as she sat down, her thoughts crashed off into the distance. The hymns and readings were like waves beneath an empty sampan. The body she left behind was as still as the long prayer pews.

October came, and the shipping routes from the north wrapped around her ankles, constantly pulling her toward the docks. She knew all the ships by heart. There were many that Pastor Chiu could have taken—he could have left from Amoy, Honshu, Tamsui. If he missed all of those, there was always the sailing from Manila at the end of the month.

All month long, she paced distractedly through Sandakan's narrow alleys. Her shoes seemed to decide the route. Some mornings, she would set out for the pasar and find herself walking along the high street to the port. Her head was filled with the lost clacking of her geta. She would come to and find she had gone too far. Those long, drooping rain tarpaulins, the damp walkways, the wood factory with its whirling sawdust, the baskets of dried seafood, the oxcarts that reeked of manure—they had risen like a cloud of dust, then vanished.

In the afternoons it usually poured, and her waxed umbrella was heavy. Gray clouds clustered over the harbor. The docks were in chaos. The Japanese wanted Shandong, and a Chinaman spat at her for it. Why blame me, she wondered. There were so many Chinamen. Coolies, yelling and unleashing fists into the rain. She understood most of what they shouted. Even if she hadn't, she would have known those two most important syllables: *Ja. Pan.*

They won't hurt me, she tried to reassure herself. They can't.

Bundled sacks of Manila hemp were piled beside the lane for loading carts, soaking from the rain. The Chinamen refused to touch Japanese goods. In front of the Dutch ship just docked from Manila, a large, bustling crowd had gathered; on the one in from Honshu, passengers pressed up against the deck railings, waiting helplessly for a gangplank to appear.

The ignored vessel was steeping in the stony blue water, rising from it like a vertiginous cliff. No longshoremen approached. Seagulls cruised through the rain, carrying with them the bleakness of the ocean. Waves sprayed foam over the outstretched stone pier. Kikuko missed Pastor Chiu and wished fervently that she had two bodies: one to leave behind in Sandakan, and another that could sprout wings and fly away.

A shoal of light and shadow flitted across the floral-patterned wallpaper and behind the drawing room curtains, where it was recast into waves. Sir Kimson had left, to attend to some mysterious business inspired by the governor general's letter. Kikuko, now fully dressed, inspected the pictures on the walls. The various incomprehensible maps held no interest for her, because they weren't how she pictured North Borneo or its surrounding sea. She perceived it as fragments, sounds, a multitude of little details: crows and sea birds, horns of steamers coming into port, debts in the grocery store, ships, rickshaws, sailors of all different races, sticky bodily fluids, and creaking beds. As for the portraits, what Sir Kimson referred to as "those blood-sucking swine" (England's King George the Fifth among them), she didn't feel like they had anything to do with her.

Well, except one.

It was by that elderly Frenchman, named Odilon, or maybe it was Adirun. She'd met him at the first dinner party she had attended at Sir Kimson's. After the dinner he got very drunk; so drunk that he wouldn't stop pawing at her, groping her all over, wanting to play the domination game that often went on in the brothel. Sir Kimson and the other guests sat in a cheerful circle around them, watching as they writhed around on the drawing room's horse-hair sofa, like opponents in a wrestling match. Afterward, the Frenchman left behind a few sketches and charcoal drawings, by way of thanks. Kikuko did not like them. They were full of giant lidless eyes and hot-air balloons like human heads, and she found them disturbing. There was only one she didn't mind: a huge hot-air balloon was drifting over a city and, beneath it, people were throwing their heads back in awe, leaving their horses to run where they liked. The steam from the balloon was like a hairy dog's tail against the sky. Sadly, Sir Kimson refused to hang that one up.

Until recently, Kikuko had always looked away if she didn't want to see. There was a picture on the wall that she especially disliked. When she asked Sir Kimson why he insisted on displaying it, he said it was a portrait like any other, just with the face hidden. It deserved to hang among the greats. One day, she told him it was like being stared at by a ghost, and he replied, "That's what turns me on."

Looking at it now, what could be seen of the face's half-exposed cheeks and beard reminded Kikuko of Jesus. Jesus hiding behind a circular opening, which could have been the window of a lighthouse or a jail cell. He was looking out, his expression that of a prisoner awaiting rescue. It was a dark, wintery painting, but the single eye burned exceptionally bright. Especially when she and Sir Kimson were in the drawing room with all their clothes off.

She felt a shudder in her spine.

But he isn't Jesus, she thought. It's wrong to think like that. That man definitely isn't Jesus.

The carriage clock by the kitchen door slowly chimed the hour and the clouds seemed to part: rays of sunlight suddenly pierced the curtain seams, brightening the room. Kikuko knelt on the Persian rug and made the sign of the cross.

He isn't Jesus, she thought, just like Sir Kimson isn't Pastor Chiu. Pastor Chiu is a man with a generous heart. Does he love me? Surely he does. He must. We are nothing alike, but that's its own kind of love, perhaps the most noble kind. This being so, I will go and love others as he loves me. This is how we will multiply, like Jesus multiplied those two loaves and five fish. I will share this love I have received with others. I will love this lascivious, brutal, foul-tempered rogue. Not only that, I will also love those who stand against him. I will love everyone, anyone who comes to me, and in this way it will be as if I have received Pastor Chiu's love.

Her thoughts carried on like this. She felt another tide of gratitude and all at once her mind was illuminated.

How miraculous, she thought excitedly, these aren't my own ideas. Someone has planted the seeds for them in my brain.

The clock stopped chiming. A steady tock-tock-tock returned to the hall. Kikuko made the sign of the cross, then clasped her hands together. "Amen."

She felt transcendent. As if she were sitting inside a flower growing toward the sky. She searched her mind for sentences that could capture this elation and settled on Psalms 4:7: "Thou hast put gladness in my heart, more than in the time that their corn and their wine increased." Psalms 139:17: "How precious are thy thoughts unto me, O God!" And then Psalms 139:3: "Thou compassest my path and my lying down, and art acquainted with all my ways." Energy coursed through her body. She felt at once powerful and profoundly relaxed, as though the gateways to her soul had been thrown wide open. It was like drinking the fine wine at one of Sir Kimson's parties.

Pastor Chiu's face and body appeared before her, only he wasn't floating in the air this time; he was reclining on the Persian rug. His cheeks were flushed, his eyes were starry, and he was unbelievably sexy. Naked like Adam, looking up at her from between her thighs.

Heat spread rapidly from the pit of her stomach, until her whole body was boiling.

"Oh God!" She leaped up and rushed to the kitchen.

The kitchen was astonishingly dirty. Fragments of broken plates were piled in the corners. Firewood that had once been stacked neatly under the stove was strewn all over the room. The sawdust covering the floor was clumpy, like a blanket of dead leaves. She tilted the clay water pot on the stove, removed the lid and started scooping the contents into her mouth, without even looking inside. The water tasted stale, as though it had been sitting there a long time, but she didn't care. It was pleasantly cool.

Then came the next part.

The butler rose up soundlessly from the other side of the stove, clutching a hammer. His face was black and his eyes were ringed with green. One of his cheeks had swollen up, turning a mottled purple. His finger was bleeding. A living dead man.

Kikuko screamed. Ran out into the sun.

She ran as fast as she could, not pausing to put on her geta. She had not been this frightened in a dozen years; she ran so fast that she was about to take off. Her hair flew out behind her and her sleeves flapped like wings.

All she could think was: don't be scared don't be scared don't be scared. It can't hurt you, nothing can hurt you.

There's only one bastard who can. He can definitely hurt me, but I'm going to love him so much…

Out on the lawn, the balloon was inflating. A perfect, shiny sphere.

The cable that tied the basket to the work platform was taut and twitching. Hans looked on in delight.

"This one, I've flown it once before, long-distance! For a little jaunt over Sandakan, oh, it's perfectly safe."

He opened the little wicker gate to the basket.

"Just don't fall into the jungle, don't let those natives—"

"Move it!" said Sir Kimson.

Before Hans could get out his reply, Kikuko had

swooped past like a bird. An enormous ball of fire erupted behind her.

And there it was: the grand residence of Sandakan's esteemed superintendent, Sir Kimson Wings, crashing to the ground. Flames leaped and half the sky turned black with smoke.

Kikuko jumped into the basket. Sir Kimson followed, slashing the mooring cable with a knife. The balloon was full of air. The grass receded. The people below were pale with fright, sliding quickly away beneath the basket, shrinking to specks. A man ran along the road like a wronged ghost, screaming, "Stop him, that conman, that fraudster—"

Said fraudster offloaded a sandbag and turned up the burner. The flame blazed golden.

Someone opened fire, but it was no use. They were too far away. A little squadron of soldiers sprang up, marching through the house as though they had been lying in wait. Red uniforms, black felt berets, moving in a perfect *V* formation. They looked like ants.

The balloon passed over impeccably ordered plantations. Rubber, coconuts, cacao. The jungle covered the hills like a rich green quilt. The branches of the Kinabatangan River weaved in and out of the undergrowth. St. Michael's church looked no different than any of the other buildings around it; they all looked like tinderboxes.

The docks. Kikuko craned her head out of the basket, looking for the Manila ship—it should have come in that day, the last arrival of the season. Where was it? The balloon continued along its invisible path through the sky, and suddenly everything was even farther away. Zinc roofs merged into terracotta roofs, lying in static waves beneath the sun.

The balloon followed the curve of the bay, then flew out over the ocean. An island like a green olive. Islands scattered like gravel. White foam seemed to spout directly from where the blue dome of the sky met the water. Kikuko was too high up to perceive the waves: all she saw were white lines, rolling and dispersing, rolling and dispersing.

A tiny boat bobbed in the middle of the blue.

"Lan-ka ship! Me, me, me!" Sir Kimson's face shone with glee; he was so overcome that he could barely speak English.

"There they are, my Caos of the South Seas! My family! Come to meet me! Those red-haired devils are so high and mighty, but they can shove their ang moh heads up their assholes, this dogshit ping-bong is all mine now!"

He threw his head back and laughed.

He tugged gently on a dangling cord, which opened the little vent at the top of the balloon, extinguishing the burner. Abruptly, they dropped to barely a hundred meters above the water.

The ship was not a pretty sight. Rotting, decrepit, loaded up with rusting copper and iron debris. All its surfaces were thoroughly blackened. Men and women were milling about. It didn't seem like a freighter, but it hardly seemed like a fishing boat either.

Kikuko thought of rumors she'd heard about cruel, unfeeling pirates, especially the notorious Caos, and felt the hairs on her arms prickle. The ship was close now, and the people on board were shouting. The man she had known as Sir Kimson shouted something back and they tossed out a rope. At the end of the rope was a devilish hook, which glinted in the sunlight—a few moments and it would land in the basket. Kikuko offloaded a sandbag and fired up the burner. The balloon shot up. A transformation took place among the people on deck: they screamed and yelled at the top of their lungs.

Their voices gradually fell away.

"Shitting, shitting fuck!"

The wind blew, carrying the balloon along with it. They were not as high up as before. Soon, they were back above Sandakan. Soldiers scuttled along the narrow alleyways, every so often firing up at the balloon. Kikuko could see the sparks at the ends of their rifles.

"You're going to get us killed," she said.

"Not so easy," said the rogue. "The northeasterly is coming."

"You think you're so clever," said Kikuko.

"Mong-gang! You stupid cunt! I was born on the seas. That devil bastard they called Sir Kimson is dead and gone. They know I'm a pirate now, and as you're with me, if they kill me they'll kill you too."

"*Atama okashi!*" said Kikuko, reverting to Japanese. "Get out of the way!"

"How can I get out of the way? Leave that sandbag!"

Kikuko wanted to shut off the burner. Once again, she and Sir Kimson were tangled together, ready to tear one another apart. To Kikuko, wrestling like this felt like embracing herself. The sun was blinding. A bright halo flitted before her eyes, making the pirate look not quite real, like a figure from a dream. At certain moments, he seemed to disappear completely. Then the basket would turn and the halo would vanish, the shadows would settle, and he'd come back into view. But even then, she wondered—is this an illusion? Who is he really?

She bit him. He roared in pain and slapped her across the face. That brought her to her senses. All she had wanted was to give thanks, receive blessings, love. To love and be loved, to hold and be held.

When the basket spun, its suspension cables became tangled up with the rope for the vent. Somehow they stayed up, their lives at the mercy of that bundle of rope. As dusk fell, they headed into the sea of clouds along the horizon. Islands drifted through it, the wind carrying them in from the distance, the whole sky an expanse of ink-blue ocean. Thousands of waves seemed to bat clusters of islands toward the shore, then pushed them away, then new waves rolled in from the distance and began all over again. In this way, the islands never met the shore but neither did they leave it. They were near then far, near then far, on and on, in an endless rhythm.

Kikuko knew what happened to bodies without shells. They frothed, turned into clouds, then into smoke. But sooner or later, so did the tough ones. Shell or no shell, they all turned to smoke in the end.

The horizon whirled, sketching an enormous circle. The setting sun turned the jungle a wildfire red.

The northeasterly arrived, and it blew them out to sea. Perhaps because the hot air was starting to fail, or perhaps because it was October, sometimes they drifted gently, and other times they jerked violently from side to side, like a quick-stepping dancer. They were in a wicker basket two hundred meters up, floating up and down, weaving back and forth across the shoreline. When the balloon dropped, the abruptness was shocking: for a moment it felt as if they were already dead, plummeting into the sea from the heavens.

Until the fall stopped, and the balloon rose again.

Kikuko felt the weight return to her body. The pirate was solid again. His bones knocked against hers, his joints against her breasts, shoulders, waist, backside, thighs. It hurt, but at every collision she felt a pang of desire.

Her shoulders trembled. From her head to her feet, she frothed like whisked batter. Her stomach was cramping intensely. She couldn't control it, it was simply too bad, and even if they were about to die, she still had to—now—right now—

"Filthy whore!"

"It's your water that's filthy! What kind of trickster is so stupid he couldn't leave one maid behind?"

"No point! If I'd known this would happen, I'd have sent the butler to the pig house and got a pig to fuck him so hard his balls ended up in his ass."

"But what about the cooking, boiling the water?"

"I kept a whole house of them and I used one a day, then I killed them after. The day before yesterday I'd finished the whole lot, and yesterday no one came to serve me—goddamn it, you stink! Couldn't you at least die first?"

Shit the consistency of watery porridge dripped through the basket, falling on—well, who knows where the wind took it. Fortunately, the rain came, slicing through the blue of the sea and sky. The balloon dropped and the waves were suddenly so close that they threatened to carry off the basket, but then the descent stopped again, thanks to the razor-sharp reactions of this old pirate by the name of Cao, who rapidly offloaded two more sandbags. The rain had skewed his fake nose and beard, making it look as though his features had been ripped off and then badly reassembled; only his chin remained in place. He added fuel to the burner and the balloon tilted, as though climbing a mountain, narrowly avoiding an enormous ship that was slicing through the waves.

Kikuko wiped rain from her eyes, striving to read the ship's name. And there it was, written out in katakana: Manila maru.

Oh God. Kikuko felt a trembling spark of hope: I beg You.

Was he there?

The deck was soaked from the rain. The balloon flew so low over the ship, it almost seemed it would land.

That's October for you, month of unruly winds and unpredictable currents. The balloon cruised slowly over the deck, where rain splattered and bubbled. It passed over the wheelhouse and chimneys, and steam from the latter might even have dried the bottom of the basket a little; might even have pushed it higher up. Deckhands and steerage passengers watched a whale-like shadow move over their heads. A shadow huge enough to crush them and, even through the downpour, a shadow that howled like the sea.

March in a Small Town

"The girls wielded their scissors with great zeal, cutting out their clothes patterns."

— Xiao Hong, "Spring in a Small Town"

TWO YEARS EARLIER, nimble of hand and foot, bare soles smacking across the floor, Cui Yi had been able to run through all ten rooms without even pausing for breath. Ten was not so many, but it was a tall, thin, four-story building without an elevator. During the day, the hallways of the second, third, and fourth floors were lit by a couple of dim lamps. The wallpaper was old and floral-patterned, with damp patches and scuff marks faintly visible beneath the windows and along the base of the wall. Two Malay maids were in charge of cleaning the place, and had been for over twenty years.

Seeing as Cui Yi was there, her aunt gave her the task of running up to inspect the rooms as guests were settling their bill, to make sure the towels, slippers, mats, drinking glasses, teapots, and so on were all accounted for. They were hardly high-quality items (the insides of the teapots were black with stains, and the flush toilets and desk lamps were always breaking), but that was no guarantee.

Once, a guest had walked off with the light bulb.

"People do the strangest things," said her aunt.

The guesthouse was near the bus station, indicated by a sheet of galvanized iron hanging from the ceiling of the five-foot walkway, featuring white lettering on a painted blue background. When the bamboo shutters were pulled down against the sun, it was not uncommon for bird nests full of eggs to come down with them.

There was a rickety wooden staircase on one side of the lobby. At each turn in the stairs, a louvre window looked onto the pasar; early every morning, sunlight splashed through the slats. Cui Yi used to charge up those stairs, taking them two or three at a time on her way back down. She didn't worry about the wood giving way—if it did, that would be her passage to a whole new world.

This particular year, Cui Yi had arrived in February. Her cheeks had filled out, although the rest of her was still skinny, and she wasn't as quick on her feet. The stairs felt narrower and her feet seemed to have grown. She climbed slowly now, taking one step at a time.

Every so often she sat with her legs up behind the reception desk, painting her fingers and toes with her aunt's nail polish. She copied her aunt's way of nestling the phone in the crook of her neck and greeting callers with an affected, sing-song, "Nam Tin Guesthouse…" When there was nothing to do, she picked up a newspaper, usually either *New Life Post* or *Mun Sang Poh*, and went to sit by the door, reading the serialized novels. She liked the feng shui and palm- and face-reading sections too, and would go examine herself in the mirror, or flip over her hand to inspect the lines. Even her aunt couldn't resist joining in with that—she would reach over with hers, asking when she was due to strike it rich in the lotto. Three of her aunt's fingers were adorned with sparkling rings, and there was a grotesque tattoo of the character 恨 on her wrist. *Regret.* The strokes on the left-hand side, supposed to represent the heart, were oddly squashed. "Didn't it hurt?" Cui Yi asked once. And her aunt replied, "The heart part did."

The first Saturday in March, Cui Yi helped style her aunt's thick hair into a beehive, just like Jenny Hu's. She stabbed it full of bobby pins, securing the structure from every side. When the bell rang at reception, she had just painted on the first of her aunt's eyebrows.

"Damn it," grumbled her aunt. "Trust them to show up now, right when I'm in the middle of something."

"I'll go," volunteered Cui Yi.

"My ass you will," said her aunt, and strode to the front desk.

In the bedroom mirror, Cui Yi could see through the reflected doorway to the reception area beyond. Her aunt's hair looked beautiful, like a big black conch shell. Her backside was even more impressive, a fact all the more apparent because she was standing up and shifting impatiently behind the desk, causing her buttocks to jiggle from side to side.

The figure at the desk had his back to the light, and an expression gloomier than an overcast sky.

Cui Yi watched her aunt turn away from the desk and yell, "Ah Cui!" She was staring right at her, looking through the door and into the mirror.

"Ah Cui—"

"Coming!" shouted Cui Yi, not moving an inch. She had a perfect view of the guy from where she was. He couldn't have been more than a few years older than she was.

"I'm taking him up, watch the desk," said her aunt.

Cui Yi stared as he moved away from the desk, and everything returned to being blank and lonely. She went to sit in the lobby. The idiot next door was singing again, *Titti titti, little titti titti...* He was always inside, behind a shadowy, grate-covered window that faced onto the street. He only sang for the Indian; that was how you knew the Indian was back. The Indian never wore a shirt, only pants, and his hair was matted into coarse, rope-like dreadlocks. The singing had no effect on him and after a while the same was true of Cui Yi, who often found herself listening without really hearing. Today she sat in a daze, watching the comings and goings in the street, her thoughts flitting like mosquitoes, and she couldn't have said when exactly the idiot stopped.

Cui Yi moved back to the bedroom and slumped across one end of the dressing table, head in her hands. Her aunt's slippers slapped down the stairs. Her face slid into the mirror.

"Don't swing your feet, it's bad luck," said her aunt. "Want to come out with me?"

Cui Yi slowly shook her head.

There was nothing left for her to help with. Her aunt put on eyeliner. Cui Yi heard someone in the lobby and, in the mirror, watched the guy leave through the front door.

Sometime after six thirty, her aunt was finally ready. She had cloaked her generous body in a full-length dress of gold brocade, which swished around as she admired herself in front of the mirror.

"How do I look?" she asked. "Classy?"

Cui Yi grinned, then nodded.

The evening mist had turned the street soft and golden. The surface of the street was slick as a fish's back. Her cousin Ah Feng sat behind the reception desk, watching a football match on a little television set. He had both arms flung wide and propped casually behind his neck, revealing luxurious clumps of underarm hair.

No one came in. Cui Yi was bored out of her mind. The light faded and mosquitoes hurled themselves against a halogen light in the five-foot way. Rain swooped in from the distance, as if all the town's roofs were one broad mountain summit. The loudspeakers at the end of the street struggled against the downpour, their songs cutting in and out. Across the street, a shopkeeper unhooked a display of schoolbags with a long pole. Boxes of goods were dragged inside. Cars sped past like ships slicing waves. Every so often, the intense black of the sky was rent apart by a flash of lightning, illuminating the line of the clouds and mountains.

Before it was even ten o'clock, Cui Yi yawned and went to collapse in her aunt's bedroom. It rained all through the night, pouring one moment and easing off the next, sending water gurgling through the drains that wrapped around the building. The house felt as if it were overrun with frogs. Cui Yi brought her knees to her chest, curling up under the quilt, and in her dreams the house rocked like a train carriage full of frogs.

The next morning, the guy came down to pay his bill. As usual, Cui Yi went up to check the room, assessing the situation with one expert glance. It was on the first floor. There was one big window, which was covered in a mosquito net and overlooked a junction. Cui Yi could see the traffic lights on the island in the middle, and a dotted white line that stretched on and on along the pavement, until it disappeared into the distance along with the cars and the buildings.

Something had fallen under the dressing table. It was about the size of a stamp. Cui Yi picked it up but still couldn't tell what it was; after examining it for a while, she established that it was thicker than a stamp, more like a pebble worn down by a river. She rolled it around in her palm, feeling as though she could crush it with one hard squeeze of her fist. Then, in a rush of tenderness, she tucked it carefully into her pocket.

At the bend in the stairs on her way back down, the light through the window slats scattered her shadow across the steps.

"Took you long enough," said her aunt.

Cui Yi did not have the energy to reply. Her legs gave way and she sank down into the shadows behind the front desk. The wood was sturdy; she could see the eyes and whorls of its grain, the lines pulling and stretching until they slackened and merged, fixing in wave after congealed wave. A drawer opened. Her aunt pulled out a few ten-ringgit notes and passed them over the counter.

Morning sunlight bounced off the cement floor, making Cui Yi's eyes smart.

"What's your problem?" asked her aunt.

"I'm tired," she replied. "My legs are tired, my head is tired…"

Her aunt opened the account book and jotted down some figures, then turned to inspect the room keys hanging along the back wall. She did this periodically. So did Cui Yi. It was perfectly obvious which ones were left, but they still had to go through the whole tedious process of making sure. Maybe one day there would be a mistake, or maybe one would disappear; who knew.

For dinner they had takeout chicken feet loh mee, slurped in the dining room. The room was submerged in a pool of gray; when there were no guests around, her aunt kept the lights off to save electricity. Cui Yi felt as though their eyes and faces had been diluted, turning into granules and dispersing through the dullness of the afternoon, pixellated. On rainy days, the gray-green walls were still and cool, and she felt like one of those birds that stop flying in winter. Movement dropped to the bare minimum, body hunched up, ears alert. Her aunt spoke in the soft, high-pitched voice of a young girl.

"When I think about what that uncle of yours…"

After dinner, her aunt would always start reminiscing, lamenting her hardships. Soon she'd move on to crooning a few gloomy lines from her favorite song: *All day wiping tears away… like a dream all gone astray…*

Since her exams, Cui Yi had felt nothing but infinite exhaustion.

Ah Feng always slept during daylight hours. He woke up every so often for a bowl of noodles, or to light a cigarette and read a few pages of a martial arts novel, but quickly fell back asleep. He was a night owl. This worked out very well, as Cui Yi and her aunt could watch the desk during the day and let him take over in the evening. The main entrance was locked at midnight, but there was a side door by the stairs, which guests could access with their keys.

Cui Yi had lost track of how many times she had flipped through the paper: Lee San Choon's glorious rise, a Guanyin sighting, another report about zombies buried on the beach. Even the lucky number forecast was emblazoned on her memory. Without intending to, she nodded off.

"If you want to sleep, go and do it in the bedroom." Her aunt's voice sounded garbled and full of echoes, as if coming from inside a vat of water.

"Mmm," she replied.

The street swept through her dreams like a tide.

When she woke up, her neck and shoulders were stiff. Her aunt was listening to the radio. "The time now is five minutes to three o'clock," said the female presenter. Cui Yi wiped saliva from her mouth. The doorway was dark.

"I'm going into the back for a minute," said her aunt. "Keep an eye on things."

"Mmm," said Cui Yi.

The sky was overcast again. A young man stepped into the lobby.

Cui Yi looked up in surprise. He had the same luggage as before, with the addition of an umbrella.

"I need a room," he said.

Cui Yi should have called her aunt, but she didn't.

"Let's see your ID," she replied.

He took it out. She opened the register and noted down the details.

"Same room as yesterday?" she asked.

"Huh?"

"The one you left this morning, do you want…" she trailed off.

It was the same bad-weather face as the previous day, but the eyes behind his glasses displayed no recognition at all. What does he take me for, she thought—the idiot next door?

She waited briefly but her aunt didn't return, so she locked the cash drawer and led the guy upstairs. This was not allowed; her aunt had forbidden her from showing strange men to their rooms. But this one wasn't much older than she was. They walked past the room overlooking the junction, number 102, where he'd stayed the day before. He made no comment. She opened the door to room 103, turned on the light, and left.

She turned back at the top of the stairs, noting the line of light that crept out from inside the room and gradually faded into the gloom of the corridor.

The rain came back in the afternoon. It hammered down with a force that seemed capable of cracking rocks. The five-foot way was a glistening sheet of water and the drains bubbled like anxious brooks. The gas delivery man dashed in, wearing a pale yellow rain suit. "Hey, Ma'am, pay up, quick, quick"—the words rubbed against one another, folding up and pressing close, becoming soaking wet and tangling up, sucking each other in, rustling past, and tearing wide open. Water sloshed in boots, on sidewalks, in plastic bags; everything was amplified. Outside, people huddled in the five-foot way, chattering, occasionally popping a head through the door to look around. The deluge scoured roofs and sewers.

At half past three, the guy came downstairs and went out, umbrella in hand, face still stony.

Cui Yi's aunt was in the tea lounge, singing into the enormous full-length mirror. *Ah... Love is like fog, love is like flowers... my foolish flowers.* She loved to sing and would carry on even when guests came in for tea or a cigarette, absorbed in her own performance. If anything, having an audience only encouraged her. The guests clacked their applause. The ground was thick with peanut shells.

"Back in Melaka, on stage at the Milky Way nightclub, oh, they loved me—the Indians, the Singaporeans, it didn't matter, they all came backstage looking for me, sent me flowers, so many flowers that... oh, even my dreams smelled sweet!" she proclaimed. "The Japanese loved me too. They said I was Melaka's Theresa Teng."

Cui Yi sat beside the dish cupboard with her grandmother, Ah Nei; Cui Yi on a little stool, Ah Nei in a rattan chair. Cui Yi wore a pair of soggy wooden sandals. Both she and her aunt had bright red toenails. The skin of Ah Nei's big toe had cracked and cleaved in two, and half was turning black; she blamed her nails, saying they were sharp as razors. Wherever Ah Nei went, her wooden sandals went too. She was only staying for a week, then she was going to pack them up and head north to visit her eldest daughter.

She listened distractedly to her third daughter's rendition of "Sayonara." If a butterfly flew past, she'd have paid it the same half-hearted attention. Cui Yi often wondered how a woman like that could have given birth to a daughter like her aunt. Then again, none of Ah Nei's children were much like her, other than her eldest.

"Were there any good Japanese?" asked Cui Yi, knowing Ah Nei had lived through that time. She was very old.

"Of course," said Ah Nei. "What else would they be. They fought off the Malays. They saved us."

She said that once the family had had to flee in the middle of the night, and made it as far as Brickfields, where two Malays made off with the cloth they were carrying with them. But, lucky for them, they bumped into some Japanese soldiers, who got it back.

If Cui Yi hadn't asked, Ah Nei wouldn't have brought it up. She had no interest in talking about a past no one else knew about; she only cared about family gossip. Failing that, even ants were of greater importance to her: the cupboard legs were each set in a bowl of water, and from time to time she would crouch down to monitor the water levels.

There were a few elderly guests in the lounge, their faces as wrinkled as steeped tea leaves and their voices hoarse from tobacco smoke. Cui Yi's aunt seemed impervious to them, her voice ringing clear through the room. She sang for herself, but the guests seemed to enjoy following along.

At eight o'clock, the guy reappeared, squeezing through the wall of people sheltering in the five-foot way. He skirted around the bucket of mandarins beneath the window, went through the side door, and headed upstairs.

Outside the front door, the evening rain had dyed the street as ink-blue as the back of a whale.

Cui Yi glanced at the clock. It wasn't quite eight. Days were long and nights were short. Her mother often sighed over this. "While there's life, there's work." In all the weeks she'd been staying with her aunt, this was the first time Cui Yi had thought of her mother.

All night long, the rain pattered and the frogs croaked.

Five guests checked out the next morning, meaning five trips upstairs to inspect their rooms. The earliest departure was an old man who'd stayed for two days. When she entered his room, the sun was only just gracing the rod at the top of the curtain liner, casting weak ripples across the ceiling. The Malay cleaning ladies threw open the window, letting the street noise flood in, then started beating the pillows to get rid of the mildew and cigarette smoke.

Wednesday again. The *Mun Sang Poh* landed with a slap.

When the guy came to check out, Cui Yi's aunt was in the bathroom. Cui Yi should have told him to wait, but he looked so impatient that she took his key and deposit receipt, opened the cash drawer, and gave him back his forty ringgit. She didn't even check the room, just let him go.

It was still before noon.

Cui Yi browsed the *Mun Sang Poh*. More party disputes. A ghost in the Genting Hotel. A ghost in a school bathroom. Ah Feng had left a half-read novel under his canvas chair; Cui Yi picked it up and started leafing through it, just to kill time.

One o'clock, lunch. Two o'clock, shower.

Three o'clock and the sneakers were back, although their owner acted like it was the first time. He carefully examined the price list beneath the counter glass.

"How much for your cheapest room?" he asked.

What was his problem?

While she considered the question, her mouth robotically recited the requested information: "Single room without bathroom is twenty-five, with bathroom is forty, twelve o'clock checkout."

She took his ID, made a copy.

"How many nights?" she asked, following the usual protocol.

"One."

Her aunt was fast asleep in the canvas chair behind the desk. Her mouth kept dropping open, erupting into snores and incomprehensible sleep-talk. The arrival of a new guest had failed to rouse her. Cui Yi turned to select a room key from the wall—105 this time—and, clasping it in her palm, went to climb the stairs.

The room's window was blocked by a building. It was darker than the last two. The guy entered without comment. Closed the door.

Cui Yi returned to reception, where she resumed her perusal of the *Mun Sang Poh*. In the Genting Hotel, you should absolutely never open the cupboard doors all the way, or you'd leave no space for the ghosts to hide. Her arms ached. They trembled on and off while she was holding the paper, though not because she was scared.

Her aunt loved the stage and was going to Melaka at the end of the month to perform with the Mayflower singing troupe. This meant Cui Yi would have to go home. She tried to imagine what would happen if she didn't—if her aunt wasn't there and it was just her and Ah Feng, what would they talk about? As children they'd been close, but over the past couple of years had grown apart. Cui Yi missed two years because she was cramming for exams, and when she finally came back, Ah Feng was gloomy and withdrawn, a completely different person. Once he'd locked up the front door for the night, he went out until three or four in the morning. If she ever happened to brush past him, in the kitchen or on the way to the bathroom, Cui Yi felt her neck shrink into her shoulders. One evening, she came out of the bathroom and saw him stirring malted chocolate into milk. She froze, unable to step any closer. He seemed to sense something too—he immediately picked up his drink and walked off, without even glancing at Cui Yi.

He was just like his father. More and more so.

Half past three, and sneakers brushed the doorstep. The guy had gone out again. No umbrella this time. The sun was in full force and the five-foot way glittered like the sea.

The two lower drawers of the reception desk were for items left behind by guests. Newspapers and toothbrushes went straight in the trash, but diaries, shoes, clothes, cosmetics, umbrellas, and the like went into the drawers; some had been languishing there for six or seven years. Cui Yi pulled out an abandoned novel. It had no cover, and no indication who the author was. She opened it at random somewhere in the middle and found a stream of sickly dialogue. For decades, the protagonists had endured long journeys, traversed whole continents, gone back and forth like those migratory birds and fish that move between the northern and southern hemispheres... The end remained a mystery, because after page 300 all the rest of the pages had fallen out.

The weather could shift in an instant. Rain came out of nowhere in the afternoons, arriving as a flood, threatening to submerge the town. It drenched the towels drying on the side of the courtyard. You had to be quick with the waterproof awnings. Cui Yi pulled the strings taut, looking up at the tiny rollers above her head.

The guy came back dripping wet and raced up the stairs like there was a ghost on his heels.

Thursday morning. The *New Life Post* at the foot of the roller shutter over the front door. Cui Yi's aunt went out to pick up wanton mee for breakfast. Ah Feng was there and, as always, he and his mother bickered across the table.

"You don't understand anything," said Ah Feng. "All you ever do is sing."

His mother was instantly furious.

"Oh, and you're so clever, are you? Haven't even passed your SRP, and already you're thinking of an MBA? They're filling your brain with shit..."

Ah Feng stormed out and raced away on his scooter, spewing white exhaust fumes down the street.

"Better off raising pigs," said Cui Yi's aunt. She went to wash the dishes.

The sky was cloudy and dark. It hung low, filling the house with a heavy gray light.

Three o'clock, the guy again. Cui Yi noted that his clothes were still spotlessly clean and neatly pressed. She handed him a key but didn't show him to the room this time.

"I'll leave that to you, sir," she said. Her right arm and leg felt like underwater seaweed; they wouldn't stop shaking.

Him again. And again. He always checked out before noon and returned at three o'clock. No one notices him but me, thought Cui Yi. Her aunt continued her inspections of the keys hanging on the wall, ensuring they matched the entries in the guest register. How had she missed this? Had she really not noticed that Cui Yi was checking in guests behind her back?

The second Wednesday in March, a *Mun Sang Poh* day. Cui Yi couldn't bear the uncertainty of the situation; it rolled through her in bone-chilling waves, traveling from her shoulders down to her toes. When the guy handed her a fifty-ringgit note and she passed him back his change, she only just resisted the urge to reach out and grab him by the neck, to check if he was really there.

"One, two, three… Sorry, we don't have any small bills," she said.

Eight 50-sen coins, seven 20-sen, sixteen 10-sen. She counted them out in front of him, then scooped them up and let them clatter into his outstretched hand.

She added the three single notes on top, folded small. His fingers were barely visible beneath the coins, but he managed to hold the bills in place with a fingernail as he walked off.

The second Thursday in March. At half past three, the guy went out carrying an umbrella. And so Cui Yi did too, trailing him like a detective.

Sunlight pummeled the street and the pavement gleamed. A warm March breeze carried off newspapers. The guy drifted as aimlessly as a ghost. He paused by the entrance to the Odeon but didn't buy a ticket. Instead, he paused and sat on the railing that ran along the sidewalk outside.

Cui Yi sat in a coffee shop in a nearby alley, drinking cold corn milk. Even once all her ice had melted, he was still on the railing, hunched over like a prawn. *Ai*. She shouldn't have ordered an iced drink on her period; her stomach would cramp. If it got bad, her arms and legs would start cramping too.

He left, she followed. He got hungry and stopped for noodles.

In front of a red mailbox, as he was crossing the road, he paused and looked around. Cui Yi instantly turned to examine the window behind her, in which Joey Wong smiled winsomely beneath an umbrella.

A bus turned into the road, blocking him from view. Huge writing, blue and yellow stripes, sliced through the reflection in the glass. Had anyone seen her following him? Cui Yi passed the shoe shop, where the woman inside never moved from her post behind the window. She felt a jolt of panic. The woman spent all day leaning on the counter with her chin in her hands; she probably saw everything.

The old granny in the grocery store was the same. All day long sitting out on that rattan chair, like a human carriage clock. Nothing got past her. She sat there fanning herself in the walkway, watching the world go by, seeing what everyone was getting up to. Who caught which bus at what time, who cycled past with who on the back of their bike, who parked where, whose license plate was noted down by parking enforcement officers, who bought what in the shops across the way and how much it cost them—any little thing like that, all you had to do was ask and, assuming she was in a good mood, she'd tell you.

Cui Yi decided not to care what the old lady might think.

I'm not from around here, she reasoned.

So she took to following the guy on a daily basis.

Every day, he would dash into a women's clothing shop. On his way down the street, he peered through all the doors, into all the shops, seeking out shadowy corners, looking at every hidden face. His route hardly varied. A left out of the guesthouse, along an alley, then onward past the furniture shop. The squeal of wood saws blended with the toneless rumble of construction site excavators, and the resulting noise sounded like someone nearby had dislocated their jaw and was screaming through their wrenched-open mouth, shaking so hard that it made their voice staccato. People walked calmly down the street or they drove their cars, completely unaffected, and the guy was just the same: day in, day out, strolling down the street.

At least, until the rain set in.

The rain interfered with his pace. When the rain came, he had to adjust to it. On days when he had an umbrella in hand, things were simpler. But still, he couldn't keep dawdling by the hawker stands, because when the rain was heavy they didn't come out, or else were too busy packing away their woks to sell anything. Instead he picked his way around the trucks and mountains of cardboard in front of the supermarket, skirting puddles and the spray of passing cars. Pressed on through the downpour, marching past the cinema, the women's clothing store, the video rental shop, the hardware shop, the bakery, until finally, inevitably ending up at the bus station ticket counter, where he would ask something and then stand staring at the timetable.

On days when he didn't have an umbrella, he might go into a shop and buy one, or buy a rain jacket, or hold a piece of paper or cardboard over his head and flap along the street like a bird, or stand like a pillar in the five-foot way, waiting for the rain to pass. He never seemed to learn his lesson from the day before; seemed always to forget how the weather changed.

Cui Yi started removing the umbrellas from his room each time he checked out.

The second drawer of the reception desk was currently home to eight umbrellas.

At three o'clock one afternoon, when Cui Yi had taken his deposit and given him a key for the eighteenth time in a row, she took out the umbrellas and piled them on the counter. Some were walking-length, others were collapsible. There were checked ones, floral ones, plain ones.

"Yours," she said. "All of them."

He looked at them blankly.

"They're not mine."

Cui Yi was silent for a moment. She felt sorry for him. "You should take one," she said. "It rains a lot here."

"Thank you," he replied. He raised his eyes to meet

hers, his gaze calm and unblinking.

"Remember to take it with you when you leave," she said.

It was an extremely wet March. Sometimes the rain waited until evening, other times the patter started at two or three in the afternoon. Like most people, if he looked outside and saw brilliant sunlight, he didn't bother with an umbrella. But the moment the wind cooled, black clouds descended like sailboats. She always trailed two or three shops behind him, observing from afar. He would freeze, lurking moth-like among the dark shadows of the goods in the five-foot way. Observing from afar, even when she had an extra umbrella, she never approached.

The umbrellas folded March into their spindly bones. It wasn't supposed to be this wet.

With every rainstorm, his route altered in unpredictable ways. But the changes were in the tiny details; there were no major surprises. Or if there were, they faded instantly from memory. He might meet an old dog by the side of the road, or stop to give an old man change for cigarettes. Or pause at the department store bulletin board to examine the "for rent" ads, causing Cui Yi to wonder whether he was planning a move. Once, he ended up sheltering from the rain in front of the old Chinese temple, where he bought a damp packet of peanuts from an Indian boy and attracted the attention of a fortune-teller. Another time, he accidentally knocked over a bicycle selling ambarellas. He crouched down and began apologetically collecting the hard, green fruits, although some were flushed away by the rain. It must have lost the vendor quite a bit of money, but when he passed by the next day, he acted completely oblivious. One day, he finally stopped just looking at the posters outside the cinema and went in to buy a ticket. This was a breakthrough. Cui Yi went to buy a ticket for herself, but sat far away from him. *The East Is Red* was showing, with Brigitte Lin swirling and flying as the invincible Dongfang Bubai. They stayed in the hushed theater as the film played on a loop. When the opening credits came up for the fourth time, Cui Yi had had enough.

A few dead leaves lay scattered on the pavement. Not even the rain could revive them. She pondered this idly as she went to buy a soda, which she drank through a straw while sitting on the railing outside the cinema, holding an umbrella in her other hand. How weird, she thought, now I'm just like him. On holiday, on holiday! A weird out-of-towner! It felt like something had happened, but nothing really had. Maybe it was just him. He had arrived to amble the streets in his haphazard, barely detectable way. If change was happening, then it was creeping into town in that same haphazard, barely detectable way: in the pockets of the street hawkers, a cinema seat, wet footprints along the sidewalk, a frog leaping out of his path (and because of that maybe the frog would bump into a lady frog, or find a few more grasshoppers to eat, or a cockroach, or ants). In Cui Yi's own memories of this particular March, she followed him and followed him as he meandered around and around the town. As if there were an impenetrable border preventing escape. There were mountains on all sides. The town was in a bowl.

From half past three until well past eight, they wandered, each clutching an umbrella.

I'm so bored, thought Cui Yi. But rereading the same old serialized novels that she'd read countless times before was boring too. She couldn't figure out his purpose. What was he looking for? Someone or something? Or nothing at all? Had he forgotten why he was there? Maybe every time he paid his bill and left the guesthouse, he did one turn around the block and forgot again?

By the fourth Saturday in March, Cui Yi had collected a total of eighteen umbrellas from his rooms. He acted exactly the same as always: he came to the desk to settle the bill, counted out his returned deposit, then picked up his luggage and left. Cui Yi locked up the cash box and slipped the key into her aunt's pocket; her aunt who was snoring away in the canvas chair.

Cui Yi opened her umbrella and trailed him through the brilliant sunshine.

He walked briskly past the pharmacy and the mini mart, did not stop at the bus station, passed by the mamak stall, crossed the river, and headed toward the train station.

Cui Yi stopped. She observed from afar as he went up to the ticket counter and bought a ticket. Then, at around half past twelve, he went through the barriers to the platform.

She stayed where she was, standing beneath a tree. There were three flagpoles beside it: one for the national flag, one for the provincial flag, and one that was empty, a boring white line standing at attention. At the side of the road, yellow trumpet flowers bloomed wide as suns.

He's leaving, she thought. The train screeched against its tracks.

Off he goes. It's all over, just like that! And I still don't understand a thing. She walked gloomily away from the train station.

Bunches of power cables tangled around the street corners, painting wobbly brush strokes against the gray sky. At some distant point along the road, a hammer was banging, steady and constant, a sound as hollow as a woodpecker in a far-off forest.

She followed the five-foot way home. In the heavy air of the pre-rain afternoon, all the merchandise was dull and gray: the schoolbags, the dangling prayer offerings, the lotto stands with red and green paper fragments strewn across the floor. Nothing raised her spirits.

It felt like her legs had shrunk. Her right foot seemed to be dragging through an endless quantity of cotton wool.

Back in the guesthouse, she mopped her sweat with wads of torn-off paper towel. Fragments stuck to her neck and chin. The fan stirred the warm afternoon air. Outside the door, the cement of the walkway was a plain of blazing white. She let her eyes droop, feeling tired.

Five to three. She stared at him in shock—like a figure from a dream, he had stepped through the doorway and walked in.

But he had no idea that he was coming back. He acted like a newcomer, leaning forward to examine the price list beneath the counter glass.

"How much for your cheapest room?"

The same sneakers, pale checked shirt, travel bag.

"The deposit is forty-two ringgit fifty," she said.

The same gloomy face as he stood with his back to the light and counted out his money. Maybe he's bringing the rain with him, she thought.

She dropped a few coins of change into his palm, brushing his fingers for the very first time. They were warm, after all.

She led him upstairs and stood in the hallway as he entered his room. Light spilled out from inside, splashing her toes.

He set down his bag and went to close the door, but her presence seemed to unsettle him. After a while, noticing that she was still there, apparently without any intention of leaving, he pulled out his wallet and offered her a coin.

She immediately fled downstairs.

At noon the next day, he once again paid his bill and left. Once again, Cui Yi followed him to the train station. This time, she stood just outside the barrier to the platform, beside a plant pot containing a luxuriant Japanese lily, and pretended to be seeing someone off.

"Here to wave goodbye? Want to come through?" asked the Malay guard at the gate.

She shook her head. The guy was close; she could see him.

He was hunched over, arms crossed. Sitting on a bench with peeling paint, looking thoroughly miserable. But where was he going? She desperately wanted to know, but there was no hope of talking to him now. His eyes were looking away, not seeing anyone. A ratty old jacket was screwed into a ball and stuffed haphazardly into the half-open zipper of his bag.

The train pulled in. She watched him board.

As the train departed, she felt herself take a step back. She had an urge to wave, like it was a required formality. She left the station, passing through the arch under the tracks. The green of the embankment was masked by a layer of fallen flower petals and dead leaves. She crossed a bridge, pausing in the middle to inspect the water below. It had come all the way from the mountains. Cement had been laid around it, turning it into a canal. Some time back, a young student had drowned in a waterfall upstream. Her body had washed down into the town, where it got stuck somewhere between the church and a Malay hawker stand. Cui Yi remembered how sad she'd felt when she first heard about it. And then every time since. Every time she thought about it, she felt that same sadness all over again.

Her right foot was numb, on the verge of becoming dead wood. Maybe I'm turning into a wooden person, she thought. A puppet! It would start with one foot and gradually spread through her body, like it did with her fourth big sister. They said it was because she had had children too young, and didn't take a convalescent month after giving birth. The whole family lived in the factory, working day and night making plastic cups for rubber tapping. The doctor said that the part of her sister's brain controlling the nerves on the right side of her body had atrophied, and that eventually she would lose all motion in her right foot. "What if she exercises more, will that help?" her mother had asked. "Worth a try," said the doctor.

But she couldn't do housework, not even the dishes. Cui Yi thought her sister's life seemed impossible, but her sister didn't seem to care; pain itself seemed to have been excised from her brain. She kept on laughing her cheery laugh, her voice booming through the dust-scented air of their factory home. Sometimes, Cui Yi wondered whether she was carrying the pain on her sister's behalf.

On every journey back to the guesthouse, Cui Yi passed the mamak stall. The golden rain tree behind it was in full flower. The yellow petals hung in drooping clusters from the branches, like fretwork lanterns. They blazed, even in broad daylight. The slope they grew on was a long way back from the sidewalk. She imagined what it would look like in the coming spring, or autumn.

Black clouds surged up from behind the tree and the rain rushed in. A thundering indigo. Once again water flooded the drains, swirled, gurgled, flowed into every tiny crevice with the precision of a fine-tooth comb, cascaded in waterfalls large and small. A thousand needles and ten thousand tiny threads ran down foreheads and into eyes, to be brushed back into hairlines. The wind swept Cui Yi's umbrella away and she watched it drift with the water for a while, before plunging beneath the surface. Her arm looked stunted and the bones in the back of her hand were splayed like a coconut palm broom. Delicate, fanned wide open, skin and flesh stretched between like frail wings. Like a fish fin. The town was small and the water was immense. Her right leg was part kite, part fish tail, but even a partial transformation was enough. She swam bumpily along the high street, past the walls and windows of shops, past a green verge like a pasture. Bump, bump, bump. She rode the water. As she passed the pasture, she saw a little girl running. "I need to escape from my mistress," shouted the little girl, but she was a long way down.

Cui Yi swam bumpily past television antennae shaped like fish bones. She felt so free.

Until fingertips drummed crisply on the counter. She started, sat up, wiped saliva from the corners of her mouth.

"Do you have a room?"

She felt like shouting. But no, she opened her mouth and her voice fled her body, fled the fan-churned air of the lobby.

"How much for your cheapest room?"

Where would the train be by now? Cui Yi couldn't even begin to understand.

"How did you get back?" she asked.

He looked at her as if she were crazy.

Half an hour later, when he walked out holding an umbrella, she followed him through the door. He was so familiar to her, but she was nothing to him. It was unfair but it didn't matter. With her eyes pinned to his back, she stumbled through the town behind him, along the same alley, the same Bank Street, past the bus station, the police station, the post office. It was all so familiar that it barely registered, as though those landmarks were just shadows flitting across water, serving only to create a path for her to follow; it was all a hazy, floating sheet of water, sometimes calm, sometimes splashed with rain. Gray pillars, shadowy shops, boxes of musty goods, frail people, old people, meek people, all passed by without a glance. Countless pillars, another alley, and then they left the shelter of the five-foot way. Rain against every available surface. It dripped off her umbrella. In a clogged drain, it beat bubbles into backed-up sewage, and the bubbles circled like flying saucers, then exploded, vanished, reappeared. He dashed into the women's clothing store and she waited outside, beneath the awning of an Indian food stand. Her legs were cold and wet. The right side of her body felt frozen but her thoughts were red hot, telling her to rub her limbs, so they would still be working when he came out again. With every step, she worried that other people would notice her. But then again, what did that matter. If they noticed, they noticed. So what. As long as he didn't. It was all exactly the same: walk, stop, rest, shelter from the rain. It was also totally different: where he stopped, where he looked, what he approached, who he brushed past. The stray cats and dogs. The film posters. A few weeks ago, Jet Li had been swapped for Bruce Willis.

Then they went back to the guesthouse. Soaked, cold, shivering.

Later, Cui Yi blamed the fever for jumbling her brain. Her whole body was burning up; her neck boiled. Raindrops smashed violently against the window awnings, drowning out any other sound. In the hallway, the foggy glow of the lamps covered the peeling wallpaper. Her right fingertips were still solid but inside they felt useless, soft as algae on the surface of a river. Soon enough, she wouldn't be able to move a single one. She unlocked the door with her left hand. That night, she'd put him back in 102, the first room he had ever stayed in.

Inside, he was asleep. The desk lamp was still on.

Some mysterious witchcraft urged her to lie down. To

her own surprise, she did: she softly lay down beside him and he did not wake up. He was asleep, maybe dreaming. Just for a minute, she thought. He won't remember. When he comes back, he never remembers anything.

"Hey," she whispered to him. "Why do you come here every day?"

He did not stir. His eyes stayed closed. She examined his face, which was resting on the red-checked pillow. He was sleeping like a child. She couldn't see his eyes, but she could see his nostrils flaring with his breath. His legs were as hairy as a gorilla's.

His palm was tucked beneath the pillow, the heel of it peeking out. She placed her own hand beside it on the bed, wanting to compare the two. She remembered something an older cousin had once said, and tried to conjure the feeling: if someone's hand makes you feel safe, that's love for you. Or, at least, a kind of love. A hint of it.

Who are you looking for?

How did you get here?

There was a shallow dip above his upper lip. She had assumed he was looking for something, or more likely someone, but maybe he wasn't. This could be a separate version of him, in the habit of searching for searching's sake. Sometimes, people carried on living even after a part of them had died. Then that dead part started to reincarnate. She had read a weird story about it once, which said it was possible for a person to meet their reincarnated self. A monk from the Gourd Temple in Balik Pulau said so too. If this was the case here, it seemed like a mystery that would be hard to crack, even if hung out in broad daylight, even if seen with one's very own eyes. Who does he look like? she wondered, and tried to think back. Trying to remember felt like looking for a waterway in a cliff constantly lapped by the tide, while the surrounding rocks and weeds looked on, oblivious. It was a mystery. Life was a mystery. So were newspapers. And the door to every room in the guesthouse; those even more so. Every sentence anyone said, tears, laughter, time, loneliness, existence. It was all a mystery. Including this matter, this moment. Especially this.

A moth settled on the lampshade. The light changed.

Is it something you can't talk about?

She turned over, feeling oddly devastated. The winter bird was dying. It was inside her stomach, shrunken like a plant's tendril, and heat and time were turning it into a fossil.

"Can I help you?" she asked. Whispering, as if talking to herself.

She went over to the window. The rain was black and she couldn't see anything. The window screen was too bright. She reached through it to the desk lamp. If I can reach through it, I must be dreaming, she thought. The moth flew away. She took the thing she'd found in his room on the first day out of her pocket. It was a chunk of stone now, the kind you might find scattered on a riverbed, rubbed smooth by the current. There were a few gray squiggles on the top, a little bit like writing but not quite; maybe it was still growing. She put it on the table.

"I'm about to go home and I'm not coming back," she said. "I know you're not here looking for me."

Her right arm tingled, and she almost fell on top of

him. Her heart thumped. He was curled up. He seemed very far away, at the bottom of a sea she couldn't access. Never mind. Everyone has their own sea. She watched over him for a while, and it was like watching the surface of water. And even though he was right there, she started to miss him. But she couldn't get any closer.

Whatever happens, I am a keeper of mysteries, not a child anymore.

If only the blue waves could wash all my sorrows away…

Her aunt's singing voice was a fragile thread, nothing like her ordinary speaking voice. It grew strained and thin at the high notes. This was bad singing technique, she'd been told; it would ruin her vocal chords. It was a long-standing source of regret. For years, she'd been singing in fits and starts. She wasn't the best singer, but still she sang.

Cui Yi wrote:

Will you come looking for me?

If you come to my house, you should know that the floor is cracked. It is cracked into many pieces and swollen in the middle, as if there's been an earthquake, but there hasn't; it's like that because of the whale.

Kedah province used to be all sea (the Kedah Sea, the Laut Kedah). One day, the sea water retreated, and all the boats suddenly dropped, crashing onto the back of a whale, and they all cracked open along the bottom. The whale had been living at the bottom of the sea for years and years, and after all that time it was covered in sand, shells, seaweed, and parasites of all shapes and sizes. Imagine: its encrusted skin was as hard as rock. After the sea retreated, my grandpa found some wood and earth and set about mending the floor. But it didn't work, because it has been cracked ever since and every few years it cracks all the way open again.

My grandma consulted the spirits of our ancestors, and according to her, the only thing left of the whale is bones. Our family isn't like other families. Ah Nei would never lie about something like that. Why should she? Unless her memory is playing tricks on her. If you ask her: Were the Japanese the bad guys? She will say: Some of them. There's always good and bad, no matter what people you are.

Last year I finished my exams. I learned two or three reference books by heart for every subject. One is never enough, because no book can tell you everything. The contents might be mostly the same, but there's always some tiny thing that's different, like one might have lots of words and simple illustrations, and another fewer words and more detailed illustrations. I learned spore diagrams, maps of mineral distribution, diagrams of frog and human dissections, cross sections of complex and single-celled organisms, electron cloud models of heavy metal atoms—and that last one amounts to dozens and dozens of diagrams. Every single thing you touch is made up of a hundred million tiny galaxies. A model of the most infinitesimally small electron cloud can be rotated and redrawn in an infinite number of ways: a figure eight, a ring of Saturn, a double ring of Saturn, layers of flower petals…it's such a complex equation. Like the mating dance of an insect, with all its seeking, posturing, and fighting rituals. Have you ever watched the documentaries on the Discovery Channel? No matter how hard you try, you'll never finish drawing those strange dances. To start with, they're invisible to the naked eye and you need a camera to put them in slow *motion. A hundred million dance moves in the blink of an eye. What are they saying, in the space of that fraction of a second?*

She mulled it over for a while. She thought about the sea no one believed in and the whale hiding under the floor. If only she could understand the silence inside the whale's belly. The floor cracked, the roof shook, bodies shook. And then something surged up. At first there were no words, just an inaudible high-pitched whistle. But where was the rumbling coming from?

"Dear listeners, it is now one o'clock."

"Aunty, I'm going out for a bit."

Cui Yi ripped out the page she'd been writing on and hid it in her pocket, then put the room register back on the shelf. As if these actions had the power to steady the pendulum in her gut. It hung there, suspended in its place, waiting for a rush of air to set it in motion again. Cui Yi felt restless, incapable of just sitting around and waiting. She wanted to scream from the bottom of her lungs.

The singing in the tea lounge reached a climax, then abruptly broke off.

"Off you go then," said her aunt.

Cui Yi walked alone past the cinema, where the wind had swept torn-off ticket stubs, straws, and candy wrappers into a pile in front of the steps. The cement floor of the five-foot way was elevated in some places and lower in others, and her feet stepped to match it, up and down, up and down as she walked. Ah Feng said things like: "It's a dead-end town, full of dead-end people."

Cui Yi didn't think that was true, although she couldn't have said what was. Maybe Ah Feng was right, but then again maybe it was just that everyone had left. Even I'm leaving tomorrow, she thought. She passed by a shop selling clocks, which forced her to glance at the time. The whole wall was covered in clocks.

Her feet dragged her past the bus station, the pharmacy, the mini mart, the three-story police station, painted in blue and white. Two Malay policemen stood chatting underneath a tree outside. Beyond the tree's dappled shadows lay a burning expanse of cement. Looking at it made Cui Yi frown and screw up her eyes.

In front of the bus station was a pool of thick black oil. I should take the train, thought Cui Yi. She pictured the pebbles beneath the tracks and the peeling metal benches on the platform. How the tracks looked so still and desolate in the rain, how at a certain point they would pause and diverge, to let another train pass. She poked her head into the furnace-like bus station and instantly everything was dark. There was light at the far end, where sun poured in through a grate over the door and fanned across the ground, scattering into endless shadows.